The watchers did not actually see the man with the leather hand draw his pistol. Instead, they saw the triple lances of flame streak from his gun barrel and slam Bert Taper's heavy body into the dust of the street . . .

Looking down at the more than fifty men squatting and standing across the hard-packed yard, Grey Taper, father of the slain man, addressed his riders . . .

"I want that gunfighter. . . . You boys see that limb? That's where I aim to hang . . . Leatherhand."

Also by Mike Wales:

LEATHERHAND #1

LEATHERHAND

#2: HANGMAN'S LEGACY

MIKE WALES

PINNACLE BOOKS NEW YORK

This is a work of fiction. All the characters and events portrayed in this book are fictional, and any resemblance to real people or incidents is purely coincidental.

LEATHERHAND #2: HANGMAN'S LEGACY

An original Pinnacle Books edition, published for the first time anywhere.

First printing, December 1983

ISBN: 0-523-42125-7

Can. ISBN: 0-523-43113-9

Cover illustration by Bruce Minney

Printed in the United States of America

PINNACLE BOOKS, INC.
1430 Broadway
New York, New York 10018

9 8 7 6 5 4 3 2 1

HANGMAN'S LEGACY

Prologue

The big man wore the uniform of a captain of the United States Cavalry. He sat deep in the hard McClellan saddle, his boot toes thrust into iron stirrups held stiffly against the big roan's front shoulders at full leg. A saber dangled on his left hip, and in a flap holster on his right, a Colt .45 army-issue revolver swung butt first and at a slight cant. The man's face was brutal, the lines of a hard past etched deeply in the sunburned skin.

Off to his right, a sergeant of cavalry rode a tall army-issue bay. He sat astride his mount with back straight and shoulders squared, his eyes roaming the desert. At his right hip he also wore the .45 so popular in the West of the 1880s. Around his waist a shell belt sagged. It held cartridges for the Springfield carbine that hung barrel down from the right-hand side of his saddle. A campaign hat with the brim turned up across the front gave the man a dashing, rakish appearance, which contrasted with the perfect, uncreased shape of the captain's hat.

The third man was also a sergeant. He had flaming red hair and sported a handlebar mustache that swept deeply down along each side of a hard mouth beneath cold eyes. His gear was a perfect match for the other sergeant's. He rode a little behind the others and led three animals equipped with heavy wooden packsaddles.

Glancing back in a proprietary way, the redheaded sergeant let his green eyes linger on the three metal boxes lashed to the packsaddles and smiled.

"Hold it," the captain suddenly called, lifting his arm. The sergeants ranged in beside him, and the three men sat their horses and quietly gazed at the wide sweep of country stretching before them.

"The Verde Valley," the redhead said somberly.

It wasn't much to look at. A long sweep of tough country hemmed in by the metallic Black Hills on the southeast and west, the tinted walls of the Mogollon Rim on the north and east, and Hackberry Mountain and the Mazatzals on the southeast.

The sergeant called Hanks rode a short distance out in front of his companions, had his look, and turned back to ask, "Captain Taper, is this where we get shed of these damn uniforms?"

Nodding his head, the captain led his men down into a nearby draw, and within a few moments they ceased being soldiers and became three heavily armed civilians riding army horses with McClellan saddles. In that country no one would pay attention to such details as army horses or saddles. Remount stock was coming and going all the time, as were the McClellans. Many men who had served in the cavalry during the Civil War had ridden home astride one. Instead of the issue Springfield carbine, the men now carried .38-40 Winchesters. The Colt .45s no longer rested in flap holsters. Now they reposed in cutaway half-breed holsters popular on the frontier during that era.

While the redhead went to the top of the draw to check the desert, the captain and the man named Hanks removed the heavy boxes from the packhorses and loosened their clasps. Walking up just as Hanks flipped the lids, the redhead whistled softly. The boxes were filled with coins.

"I'd give a lot to have been a mouse back there at Fort San Antonio and watched what happened when the pay wagon showed up empty," the redhead said.

"Get a blanket," the captain told him.

When the big man walked away, the man called Hanks remarked, "That feller, Branda, he's kinda odd, ain't he?"

"Don't ever draw on him," the captain warned.

Hanks looked amused.

When Branda returned with the blanket, the boxes were emptied in a cascade of glittering gold onto the spread cover, and the men began splitting it up in equal piles of three. An hour later they stood up and stretched and looked at their work. Hanks' eyes reflected raw greed, Branda's a kind of eagerness, and Taper's a stolidness that was unfathomable.

They repacked the coins, each man handling his own share until each had a single packhorse tethered to his saddle horn, then the captain thrust a foot into an iron stirrup and heaved his huge bulk aboard. As he mounted, the horse grunted and braced himself, then slowly shifted its weight to accommodate the rider.

"Hanks, as soon as you get set north of Jerome, you let me know," he said. "Branda, I'll expect you to have your situation well in hand in town at least as soon as Hanks gets set. Me, well, I'll take over the D-Ring-T and settle in. If we can't own everything between here and Jerome in five years we'll have robbed a pay wagon for nothing."

"Reckon Bert made it all right?" Branda asked.

"If he didn't fall down a hole," Taper said. "He just seems to get himself into one mess after another, that boy does. If his maw hadn't made me promise on her death bed to take care of him, he'd be long gone before now."

"He ain't so bad, Grey," Hanks said. "He just wants to be like his dad."

"Yeah, and it's going to get him killed someday," Taper said.

Chapter I

It began at the Red Horse Saloon. It ended in the dust of the main street of Dry Springs on a summer day so hot even the buzzards had quit circling the slaughterhouse east of town and were now perched on the roof tree, their ugly heads buried between black wings with only beady eyes showing.

The tall man had come in off the desert, watered his magnificent Appaloosa, then tied him in the alley next door to the saloon so that he might enjoy a respite from the blistering heat.

Now the man stood at the bar, a medium-cold beer in front of him, a shot of whiskey siding it, and began allowing himself to unwind slowly.

As he stood there savoring his first drink in two weeks, the blocky shape of a man appeared suddenly in the backbar mirror. The tall man dropped his hand casually to his gun butt and executed a slow turn to face a large man who had followed him through the front door.

"I know you, mister," the man said, his voice heavy with threat.

"So?" the tall man said and looked past the larger man, as if interested in something he had noticed on a far wall.

"So, in ten minutes I want you out on that street ready to go to war."

The bartender came down and said sharply, "Now, Bert . . ."

The big man held up his hand, and keeping his eyes on the stranger, repeated, "Ten minutes, or I come in after you?"

The tall man shrugged and asked, "Why?"

"Because, you're who you are and me, I don't think you're as good as everybody says you are," the man called Bert answered.

"I'm better . . ."

"Saying ain't doing." The big man went to the far end of the bar and called down, "I'll be out there in ten minutes. You be there."

"You're making a mistake, feller . . ."

Raising a quick hand, the big man shook his head. "No, just do it."

The tall man tossed off his whiskey, dropped a coin on the bar, and walked through the swinging doors, leaving them to whisper back and forward at each other.

"He'll kill you, Bert," the bartender said flatly.

"I gotta find out."

The swamper, who had been standing at the alley entrance to the saloon, carried the word.

Ten minutes gusted by while the stranger looked to his horse, then carefully checked his gun. Satisfied, at exactly ten minutes to the second he moved.

This was a quiet town made quieter now by the threat of impending violence. The feeling hung like a black squall cloud over the single dusty street. Even the mangy dog digging in the trash behind the Jinglebob Cafe acted as if he felt it, for he paused often to sniff the wind that pushed the desert sand against the side of the building.

A sudden gust spun up a dust devil and spit out a tumbleweed, sending it skittering down an alley and under a hitchrail.

The street was empty save for a big bay horse tied near the cafe and the tall Appaloosa in the alleyway.

Then the tall stranger, his brown eyes level and bleak, hitched up his gray pants and shifted the gunbelt holding the .44 Colt pistol in its cutaway half-breed holster to a more comfortable position.

At first glance, he looked like any other range rider found in Arizona in the 1800s, until he raised his right hand and tilted his hat half an inch forward. That hand was covered by an odd leather brace with straps wound around the wrist.

Dropping the leather-covered hand to his side, he carefully flicked the tiedown from his gun hammer and walked into the center of the street, where he made a slow turn to the north and stood apparently relaxed and unconcerned.

Faces showed briefly behind dust-coated windows as Dry Springs watched and waited.

A block north of where the tall man stood, the marshal's office squatted between a Chinese laundry and the town's assay office. Inside, a man wearing a badge stood gazing through the glass door, a sour expression on his face. Without turning, he spoke to a man sitting on the edge of the office's single desk.

"He'll kill him, ya know."

The man at the desk, a lean, saturnine individual dressed in black gambler's garb, cleared his throat and said, "Yep, I reckon he will."

"His paw's gonna take it hard," the marshal said and shifted irritably. He did not like the feeling of helplessness that kept him here behind the door. He would have preferred being out on the street, stopping this thing.

The black-clad man, reading the marshal's mind, said, "You can't do a damn thing, Earl."

"He's gonna take it hard," the marshal said again, then added resignedly, "there comes Bert . . ."

The man in black came to the window and watched the blocky shape of Bert Taper, his batwing chaps flapping around his legs in the driving wind, come off the sidewalk from the Red Horse Saloon in a lurching walk that was as much swagger as challenge.

He moved into the street facing the man in the gray hat, who stood stolidly in his square of ground before the hotel watching dispassionately. His eyes held a bleak sadness, for he did not want this. Shifting his weight to the balls of his feet, he waited.

As they faced each other neither man spoke. Words were wasted effort now. Action was the thing remaining to them.

"Bert's damn fast," the man in black said, but his words lacked conviction.

"Bert'll be dead in about one minute," the marshal countered, and winter winds rode the timbre of his voice.

Then Taper made his play, stabbing a blunt hand toward the butt of his .45. The marshal sucked in his breath and held it, awaiting the coming roar of gunshots.

The watchers did not actually see the man with the leather hand draw his pistol. Instead, they saw the triple lances of flame streak from his gun barrel to slam Bert Taper's heavy body into the dust of the street.

As the mushrooming powder smoke was pushed away by the gusty Arizona wind, the gunshots faded with it, leaving the tall man standing erect and alert as he watched the still body of his victim. Then he ejected the empties, reloaded, and walked to where the Appaloosa stood.

Turning, he glanced at the body, looked east to where the rising sun was just spreading its beams of light into the reflecting glass of the hotel windows, shook his head in a quick negative gesture, and stepped into the saddle.

Touching the Appaloosa lightly with the long-shanked Mexican spurs he wore, he rode past the dead man, glanced down into his sightless eyes, then up into the marshal's as the lawman stepped onto the sidewalk and nodded.

The black-clad man followed the marshal onto the walk and looked after the departing rider. "Who tells Taper his son is dead?" he asked.

As the marshal started to answer, the man on the Appaloosa turned the animal and rode back to stop before the lawman.

Nodding his head, he said, "Marshal Bowdrey . . ."

"Leatherhand . . ."

"He didn't give me no other way to go, Marshal."

The lawman shook his head and looked down the street to where a crowd was beginning to gather around the dead man and said, "I know. He always was a stubborn feller."

"Just so," the man called Leatherhand observed and turned the Appaloosa and rode from town.

The Appaloosa picked its delicate way down a rough canyon as its rider sat carefully alert, his carbine lying across the forks of the heavy stock saddle he rode. This was the Mogollon Rim country, hunting grounds for the toughest fighting men in the world, the Apache. The tall man with the leather brace on his hand had no intention of losing his hair to a marauding band of Indians.

Looking back across almost four years of hard knocks, he decided he had come a far piece since being carried wounded out of Kansas in 1878 in the jolting bed of a wagon. An old family feud had erupted in a savage gunfight. When the smoke cleared, he had lost both his brothers and the use of his right hand.

Vent Torrey, called Leatherhand because of the odd contraption he wore on his gunhand, had built a reputation as a man to stay clear of since coming west. The flesh of him had been firmed to fine steel in the farrier's fire of experience. The winds of the high deserts and the cold and bite of the jagged peaks of Colorado had left their marks on his tough, handsome face for all to see. His hands had delivered death, and it showed in the cool depths of his eyes. With it had come a legacy of bad dreams, but this too he had weathered until he was fine-tuned as a Missouri camp-meeting musician's fiddle.

He was a walker on the canyon ledge of life, playing a balancing game that had killed others and might one day kill him; but when he went down, those who knew him were making bets he would cross the river of no return with a full boatload of oarsmen to accompany him.

Now he pulled the Appaloosa up and, with a small shower of rocks and gravel rattling down the sleight incline of the trail, carefully scanned each boulder, cut bank and gully.

Nothing.

Clucking to his horse, he moved on into the canyon and followed a dry creek bed's meandering path until the narrow gap in the barren landscape opened up, presenting him a panoramic view of murderously rugged country—the kind of country even a rattlesnake would hesitate to enter, he thought darkly.

To his right, a cathedral-like spire of rock poked upward from a jumble of boulders and desert dirt, standing like some stark grave marker in a rock-ribbed land that had already killed enough men to fill a dozen cemeteries.

As he broke free of the canyon, Vent expelled softly. The cut had been a nasty trap. Now, as he rode more easily, he thought of Bert Taper lying dead in the main street of Dry Springs and for a moment felt a bleak twinge of regret. True, he hadn't sought the fight and, in fact, had tried to avoid it, but Taper wanted Vent's reputation, along with his hide. Instead, he found only death.

Vent Torrey had killed his share of men. His family had fed three generations of Torreys into the maw of a long-standing feud. He knew about the ways of violent death.

Shaking his head, he cleared it of thoughts of the dead Bert Taper and rode on.

Three days later found him just skirting the edge of some dry mountains. He was a good two miles from a low butte when he heard the first faint echo of gunfire. It was just a whisper of sound on a light desert wind, and he might have missed it if he hadn't pulled in the Appaloosa to let him blow after having climbed from a dry wash that hadn't seen water since last winter.

As the spotted horse stood spraddle-legged and snorted windily, another shot, this one just a bit louder, came to him from across the barren expanse of burned-out Arizona desert.

Vent lifted his head and keened the wind, then slid from the Appaloosa, dropped the reins, walked off toward the west, stopped and turned his left ear toward a low, rough bench and waited.

A tall, powerfully built young man, he stood with his boots planted firmly in the desert sand, and if there had been anyone in that God-forsaken part of Arizona to see him, they would have noticed first the heavy .44 Colt revolver in its cutaway holster tied to his right leg, then they would have wondered at the strange leather contraption he wore on his right hand.

Now he casually lifted the leather-covered hand and, extracting a Bull Durham sack from a vest pocket, rolled a cigarette. As he returned the tobacco and paper, he fumbled a wooden kitchen match from his hatband. Striking it on a silver-dollar-sized concho fastened to his gunbelt, he fired up the smoke just as the third shot, followed quickly by three more, came to him clearly.

Turning, he walked back to his horse and stepped into the saddle, lifted the Winchester .38-40 rifle free, and clucked softly to the now alert Appaloosa, whose ability to sense the moods of his rider had him walking as delicately as a ballerina. As the animal stepped out, Vent switched his glance from horizon to horizon in anticipation of sudden danger.

Swinging wide, Torrey came up to the north end of the butte and angled cautiously around its twenty-foot base, his body wire-tight, his eyes alert to everything around him. The rifle rode butt down against his thigh, and when he reached the turning of the cliff, he stopped and dismounted, carefully mashed the cigarette out against a large boulder, then moved catlike around the corner of the rocks, his spur rowels faint bells marking his passage.

In a low swale covering about ten acres, four people crouched among a scattering of boulders littering the ground around a muddy waterhole. Vent counted five dead horses lying in a heap near the south end of the waterhole and decided they had probably been shot right at the beginning of the fight. Looking closer, he made out a pair of boots protruding from behind a boulder, the toes pointing toward the brassy sky.

"Dead," he muttered and moved two feet farther from cover, crouching to make a smaller target. Looking south along the base of the narrow rock butte, he counted eight men lying or kneeling behind rocks at the base of the cliff, rifles pointing toward the waterhole.

"One bunch has the high ground, the other the water," he whispered to himself and moved back to his horse. Standing close to the horse's head, he mulled over what he had seen. Two groups of men were obviously in a rifle fight over the waterhole or for some other reason, but which group was in the right? Thinking about it he decided to wait.

Five spaced shots bounced their echoes off the cliff face and were answered by two shots from the waterhole. Conserving their shells or almost out, Vent thought and went back to the corner of the cliff. Hunkering down, he stuck a match in his mouth and absently chewed it while he waited, rifle across his lap.

Five minutes crawled by and Vent, not liking the hot touch of 100-degree-plus heat boring into his back, moved closer to the cliff and found a small patch of shade. He watched as the Appaloosa lifted its head and sniffed the wind, and wondered where the men at the base of the cliff had hidden their horses. Wherever they were, they were far enough away so the horse hadn't caught their scent.

"You, Wag Jorstad," a voice called from the cliff. "Leave your guns at the waterhole and I give you my word I'll let you walk out."

"Your word, Branda?" someone at the waterhole called back derisively. "We'd live about ten minutes . . . You go to hell."

"Smart fellow," Vent muttered.

"Better than dying by inches," the cold voice of the man called Branda countered.

"We got the water," the same voice called back from the waterhole.

"When you run outta shells, we'll come down and hang you," Branda threatened.

No answer. Vent decided he didn't like the sound of Branda's voice and had about made up his mind to side with the beleageured at the waterhole when Jorstad called, "You'd hang the girl, Branda?"

"Not right away," someone else called from the cliff, and the harsh sound of the voice grated on Vent's nerves. It was followed by a hollow laugh.

"Go to hell," someone called from the waterhole and Vent decided whoever it was had a lot of hard bark on him. The voice carried the tough no-quarter sound of a man who wasn't sitting in the middle of his first siege.

Moving back around the cliff, Vent stood and gazed upward at the top of the plateau fifteen feet above him. Noting the jagged breaks in the rock, he brought up his horse and stepped into the saddle, then straightened up until he was standing on the swell with less than five feet to negotiate. Squatting again, he pulled his rifle up and two minutes later scrambled over the top and began moving along a flat narrow island of rock, crouching so he wouldn't draw the fire of those at the waterhole. He moved cautiously until he was directly above the attacker's position.

"Hazen, that feller Jorstad is stubborn as 'ary any Missouri mule I ever saw," someone said.

"Dead takes all the stubbornness out of a feller," the man called Branda answered.

"Easier said than done," a voice countered.

"Don't worry," Branda growled. "We always got our ace down there. If we have to, we can use him."

A shot slammed out and was answered from the waterhole, followed by a curse and a gasp as someone took the round on the ricochet.

"Concho's plugged," a man called. "Damned bullet

bounced off the rock and nailed him right through the shoulder. He's bleedin' like a stuck pig."

Vent stood up then and, taking a long step to the cliff edge, dropped the barrel of his rifle down toward the group of riders crouched along the cliff face. "The first gent moves, I'll kill him so dead he'll think he was stillborn," he said coldly, and eased back the gun hammer.

A slim man wearing black batwing chaps, a black jacket and hat, and two guns spun around, but froze when he looked up and found the gaping bore of the .38-40 rifle pointing at his right eye. His own rifle slid from his hands and hit the rocks with a clatter.

A big man with red hair wisping from beneath his hatband and a blood-red walrus mustache cutting a bright slash above a cruel mouth turned his head and stared up at Vent from a pair of green eyes as brittle-looking as shards of jade. "Now, who the hell are you?" he hissed.

Vent smiled. "Just a feller ridin' by," he said, then added, gesturing with the rifle barrel, "best tell that waddy with the twin hoglegs, if he tries to run a sandy on me, he's gonna end up with the undertaker packing cotton up his backside, if the buzzards don't get to his leavings first."

The man with the twin guns slowly relaxed, then asked casually, "Mind if I roll me a smoke?"

"Roll away, but it'd be a hell of a note for a man to get his ticket punched just for goin' after his 'baccer."

"You, up there on the rock," Jorstad called from the waterhole. "You with us or agin' us?"

Vent kept his eyes on the now disarmed riders below him but called, "I've bought a hand on your side of the table, but I want you to tell me the name of this here game before I play any more cards . . . You hear?"

"I'm Wag Jorstad," the voice called. "Own this waterhole and a spread west of here. Feller you got corralled up there's name is Hazen Branda. He wants the waterhole, my sister, and the ranch . . . That simple enough for you?"

Still staring at the big redhead, Vent said, "Now it's your turn," and waited, watching a squat, bandy-legged puncher carefully slide his hand around behind him. Probably had a hideout gun stuck in his belt back there, Vent guessed.

"This happens to be my waterhole," Branda said, adding, "and that's all you need to know, feller."

"Not enough to hang a man over, let alone a woman," Vent countered, then tilted the rifle and shot the bandy-legged man through the chest and watched dispassionately as the big slug slammed him back into a boulder and then bounced him off its face, leaving him sprawled on his side with his legs drawn up. A pistol slid from his slowly relaxing hand.

"Damn," the black-clad man said.

"He probably will be," Vent replied.

"What happened up there?" Jorstad shouted.

"Had to kill one of these fellers," Vent called back. Silence answered him.

"You'll never live long enough to get outta this desert," Branda promised bitterly.

"If I don't, you won't," Vent said softly.

"You can't get us all," the black-clad one said, dropping his hands until they hung just off his gun butts.

A gaunt rider with washed-out blue eyes and a shiny bald pate gleaming from the front of a pushed-back hat said quietly, "Better not, Von. I know this feller."

Something in the rider's voice turned Branda still. He carefully looked Vent over, letting his eyes linger on the leather-covered right hand for a long minute, then said softly, "And so do I. His name's Leatherhand, and he's had his share of men for breakfast . . ."

The rider in the black chaps smiled. "Well, well. So you're Leatherhand. Heard they killed you over Sonora way . . . or was it Sedalia?"

"Neither one," Vent said, then lifted the rifle barrel and, nodding south, asked, "horses down there?"

Branda, not liking his position but knowing there was nothing he could do about it right then, muttered, "They're down there."

"Then shuck your hand guns and mosey off down that way. I'll be following you from up here, and when you get to the horses you leave three behind."

"What the hell for?" the man called Von snapped.

"You killed those folks' horses. You leave 'em horses. Simple."

Branda carefully let his gunbelt drop and then waited as the rest of his men followed suit. Defanged now, he led them south as Vent catfooted along the cliff above them.

Ten minutes later he watched as they rode out of the depression heading toward a deep cut in the cliff face to the south, then he climbed down the back side of the bluff and rode to the waterhole. He found three men and a woman standing looking down at the body of a fresh-faced boy, his skin already taking on the marble hues of death.

Looking around at Vent, Jorstad said softly, "He rode with us since he was twelve. Now I gotta tell his maw I got him kilt. Damn!"

Chapter II

The riders came from line shacks and cow camps. Mounting swiftly they rode for the D-Ring-T Ranch at a sharp canter. Others broke away from horse herds and cow drives and pushed already tired horses over the rough Arizona desert country, heading for the dog's-tail end of the great Verde Valley.

These were hard-faced men, the kind of men needed to raise and nurture cattle in a country that was mostly cactus, rattlers, Apaches, and outlaws. They were not gunfighters, but some of them had faced other men and watched them die through the curling gunsmoke and ridden away to remember it around campfires on the long cattle drives to places like Wichita and Dodge City, Kansas, and other points east. They were men loyal to a fault, and now the owner of the brand they rode for had called them in and they came without question.

Marshal Earl Bowdrey sat in his office chair, legs tilted back and shoulders solidly against the wall. He watched the riders swing into town from off the blistering desert, tie their hard-used horses at the hitchrail in front of the Red Horse Saloon, climb stiffly from their saddles, and tramp across the wooden sidewalk to push through the swinging doors. In his mind's eye, he could see them lining up at the bar, gulping their dust-cutters, and then back outside again where they would lead horses to the town waterhole and allow them their fill before they mounted once more and rode for the D-Ring-T.

Watching them enter and leave the saloon, the marshal thought, men bent on killing don't sit long at their drinks.

Far to the west, five riders broke from a low cut at a driving run, firing over their shoulders as they dashed into the open plain. Behind them, bent over the necks of tough little desert horses, eight supple-bodied Apaches slowly gained on the fleeing riders. Then the lead Apache lifted an old Sharps buffalo gun, aimed it carefully, and fired.

The last rider in line grunted, swayed, and rolled from his horse. Crashing to the ground, he bounced over rocks and brush and finally came to rest against the base of a barrel cactus as a wild series of shouts rose from the Indians.

As they galloped past the down man, one of them lifted a heavy dragoon pistol and fired a shot into the man's back.

A mile further along the flat expanse of desert, one of the riders got off a lucky shot and the rifle-wielding Apache traded his life for that of the man he had killed. As he hit the ground and rolled end to end, a volley of shots tore into the Indian ranks from a group of riders in a narrow canyon to their right, and five saddles were suddenly empty. The remaining two Apaches broke and rode for their lives. They were not fast enough. Two well-placed shots unloaded them into the dirt.

As the two groups of cowboys came together, a tall man wearing a calfskin vest pulled in his horse and, glancing at the sprawled bodies, remarked, "Eight good Apaches."

"Ernie Daltz bought it," a heavyset rider with Texas in his voice said.

"One of you boys catch up his horse and get him on it. Pick up the Injun ponies and bring 'em along . . . probably stolen," the man in the vest ordered and watched as a rider broke away and, with the dead rider's horse in tow, rode back after the body. A few minutes later he returned with a still form draped across the saddle. The man in the vest glanced at the body, looked up as the Indian ponies were ranged alongside them, and said, "Let's ride," and led the men southeast toward the D-Ring-T Ranch.

In Dry Springs, Bowdrey watched the gambler come along the sidewalk, a toothpick in the corner of his mouth, his clothes as neat and pressed as ever, and wondered how the hell the man kept from sweating in 100 degrees of heat while wearing a coat.

Looking at the tied-down .45 the gambler wore, the marshal speculated idly on whether he could use it or wore it for show. He had never seen Owney Sharp break leather. He had heard from others that he was very fast, but until he saw that himself, he would reserve judgment.

"Nice day," Sharp commented and, toeing a chair from the wall with a polished boot, settled into it next to the marshal. Tilting it back, he added, "For a killin'."

"A lot of men have tried to bring Leatherhand down, and somebody else always winds up riding their saddles," the marshal observed dryly.

"Maybe so, but he never had an army after him before," the gambler said.

"They tell me that Hawks family was some tougher than any army that ever straddled a McClellan saddle," Bowdrey mused.

"Grey Taper, he can put fifty men horseback," the

gambler said; and as if to reinforce his argument, three hard-looking cowboys rounded into the street from the north and trotted their horses to the hitchrail in front of the Red Horse.

"That's a good dozen that's come through here today," Sharp said.

Bowdrey, noting the D-Ring-T brands on the horses' flanks, thought, I wonder how long it will take Grey Taper to get around to me, and wished bleakly he was somewhere else.

"He'll blame me, ya know," Bowdrey said. He did not look at Sharp.

"He won't kill a marshal," the gambler assured him.

"The hell he won't," Bowdrey said and knew he was right and knew that Sharp knew it.

"Leave town. Nobody'll blame you."

"What the hell, I reckon this is as good a place as any to pack her in," Bowdrey said. "I'll hang around." He rose and nodded at the saloon. "Buy you a drink?"

As the two men entered the cool interior, the three riders bellied up to the bar turned frosty eyes their way, then looked down into whiskey glasses and ignored them.

"A bottle and two glasses," Bowdrey said and Harp Sinclair, owner and bartender of the Red Horse, pushed a bottle and two glasses onto the bar top, accepted the marshal's coin, and went away.

One of the D-Ring-T riders looked toward the table where the gambler and the marshal sat and said, "I smell me something in here. Think I'll drift on out. Never could stand the odor of skunk." He downed his drink, turned on his heel, and started for the door.

"That's far enough," Sharp said softly. He hadn't moved, but now the riders turned carefully and placed their backs against the plank; hands hanging loosely, they waited, their eyes saying nothing.

"You talkin' to me, tinhorn?" asked the rider who had started for the door.

"An apology, friend. In five seconds, or we have a funeral in Dry Springs," Sharp said. Bowdrey sighed and thought, How the hell do I get myself in the middle of these things?

"Better do it," he told the rider.

"To hell with him," the rider said and went for his gun. As he drew the two riders at the bar made their play. Bowdrey did not draw. He never had the time.

Sharp's .45 swiveled up and over the edge of the table and exploded three times so fast the roar sounded like one shot. The man in the middle of the room took the heavy slug in the center of the chest and died on the way to the floor. The rider closest to him managed to clear his front sight over the edge of his holster, then jerked sideways, piling into his partner and spoiling his aim. Sharp's third bullet caught the last rider in the stomach, jackknifing him forward and onto his face, where he lay clutching his belly and moaning in agony.

The room reeked of cordite and black smoke as Sharp rose and walked to the wounded man. Turning him over with his toe, he looked down into the rider's squinched-up eyes and said, "Wrong move, cowboy," and shot him in the face, the .45 slug hammering the man's head against the floor once as the back of his head disintegrated.

"Jesus!" Sinclair gasped. It was about a brutal a thing as he had ever witnessed.

"Dammit, Sharp, why the hell did you go and do that?" Bowdrey asked, coming over and staring down at the dead man. The second rider had taken Sharp's bullet just under the eye. Bowdrey shook his head and looked up as the gambler punched out empties and reloaded his pistol.

"Never leave a wounded man behind you," Sharp said. "If he lives, he'll come after you."

"Taper'll hang you," Bowdrey said simply.

Waving a hand, Sharp moved up the stairs, where he kept rooms, and quickly packed his meager belongings. Five minutes later, he came down the outside stairway and walked briskly to the stables. Bowdrey stepped out on the front porch and watched the gambler ride from the livery on a big black stud then gig him into a sudden gallop north.

Sighing, Bowdrey unhitched the dead riders' horses, walked them down to the livery, and turned them over to the hostler.

Grey Taper was a big man with shoulders that could be measured by the axe handle, arms that were as thick as tree limbs, and a brutal, pugnacious jaw attached to a leonine head that was granite and obsidian chiseled into shape by the jackhammer of experience. His hair was gray, had been since he was seventeen, and the lone survivor of an Apache attack on a wagon train. Now he stood on the front porch of his sprawling fifteen-room adobe house and hat pushed to the back to his head, addressed his riders.

Looking down at the more than fifty men squatting and standing across the width of the hard-packed yard, he said just loud enough for the furthermost man to hear him, "You boys all know Bert wasn't much account, and normally I'd just forget the whole thing, but he was my boy and before his maw died she made me promise I'd take care of him. Well, I failed. He's layin' inside there"—and he jerked a thumb over one shoulder—"as dead as a nit, plugged by some wandering gunfighter. I want that gunfighter."

Several men moved restlessly. Taper stared at them. "I know what you're thinking. You've heard it was a fair fight, that this shooter won square, and he even tried to give Bert a way out. Well, I know that, and it don't mean doodly squat." He lifted his arm and pointed a long finger toward a huge old oak tree standing in the center of the yard and said, "You boys see that limb? That's where I aim to hang this Leatherhand feller."

Every man there turned his head and gazed up at the huge limb thrusting out from the side of the oak.

"Now, I want six of you men to ride to Dry Springs with me," Taper ordered. "I want men who can use a gun . . . You, Cameron Spencer," he called out, and the man in the calfskin vest walked to the porch as Taper continued, "Shorty Hodge, Tuck Willoby, Vance Caudell, Smiley Brown, Cole Butram. You boys will ride with me. The rest of you break up in groups of fifteen and bring that pistol fighter back here."

"You want him dead or alive?" one of the men asked.

Taper glanced at him, then looked toward the oak tree and said, "Cain't very well hang a dead man, now can I?"

As the riders mounted and rode out, Taper turned to Cole Butram, a snaky-looking cowboy who wore two guns tied down in cutaway holsters and always walked as if he were on egg shells, and said, "Cole, saddle my horse. The rest of you boys get ready to go to town."

As the men headed for the barn, Taper tapped Spencer on the shoulder and asked, "You talked to Harp Sinclair?"

"I talked to him," he said grimly.

"What happened in there anyway?" Taper asked as he walked past his son's casket without glancing at it.

"The boys took a chaw out of something they couldn't swallow. That gambler, he was some hell on little red wheels."

"He had to be to beat all three of those boys," Taper observed. "That kid, Dancer, was fast as hell, and Marks wasn't any slouch when it came to gunwork. That's why I hired him."

"Well, he's dead now, along with two other good boys, and all because he allowed his mouth to overload his hind end," Spencer said dryly.

Stopping at an elaborate bar near a huge rock fireplace in the adobe's large front room, Taper poured them both a shot of whiskey, handed Spencer his, and lifting the glass, said, "Here's to a tight cinch and a fast horse," and drank it in one quick backflip of his wrist.

"May there always be water," Spencer countered and downed his drink.

"How long you been my foreman, Cam?" Taper asked.

"About three years, near as I can recall. Why, thinkin' of replacing me?"

Taper grinned. "Nope, too hard to replace you. Besides, you know where all the bodies are laid to rest. Wouldn't do for you to go wandering off and getting drunk. Might contract diarrhea of the bazoo."

"I ain't that dumb," Spencer said and smiled, but he didn't like the turn of this conversation.

"When we get to town, I'm going to shoot that damn marshal," Taper said.

"You figure that's wise?"

"Hell, me, I ain't got a thing agin' Bowdrey. Fact is, I sorta like the man, but if I let him live after he stood by while some damn gunfighter killed my boy, the word would travel all over this state that Grey Taper was gettin' soft. Can't have that."

"You know anything about this Leatherhand?" Spencer asked.

"Not much. Heard somewhere he was a mighty fast man with a gun."

"He's more than that," Spencer said. "He comes from down in Missouri. His family was one of those feudin' families you sometimes hear about from down in that part of the country. The way I heard it, the Torreys—that's Leatherhand's real name—and a family named Hawks just about built their own cemeteries. Over three hundred of them killed in gunfights and shootings of one kind or another."

Taper stared at him. "They any of them left, for God's sake?" he asked.

"Yep, they's Vent Torrey, his sister, who's married to a gent useta be a marshal over in Colorado somewhere. They say he's got a lot of hard bark on him too. Then they's old man Hawks. Leatherhand killed all four of his sons in one hell of a shootout. Let the old man live after mangling his hand with a shotgun."

"Know how many he's put under?" Taper asked curiously.

"They say anywhere from twenty to thirty, but you know how folks like to exaggerate. I remember killing Jim Miller over in Oklahoma. They say he murdered fifty men before they drug him outta a jail and stretched his neck, along with three other fellers."

"How the hell old is this Leatherhand?" Taper asked, pouring another drink for them.

"He'd be around thirty or close to it," Spencer said.

"You ever see him?"

"One time. It was up in Crested Butte, Colorado. He shot it out with them Hawks after they murdered his girlfriend in the middle of the street. He put two of them down that day."

"Hmmm," Taper mused. "Looks like this ain't no ordinary pistol fighter we're dealing with."

"Nobody ever accused Leatherhand of being ordinary," Spencer said as Smiley Brown came in and announced Taper's horse was ready.

As they walked out on the porch Spencer said, "Bowdrey's a good man, Grey. He's been our friend."

Grey rounded on him then and said harshly, "You think I don't know that? I still can't let it slide."

Spencer shrugged. "Might bring the federals in here."

"Let 'em come. I own Dry Springs and everything you can see from it. In fact, I own everything for a hundred miles around." Taper raised an arm and swung it in a wide arc.

"Why not just invite Bowdrey to leave the valley?" Spencer asked.

"Hell, you know he wouldn't go. He's a proud man. He'll stand and fight."

Spencer stared at Taper and thought, this time you're wrong. He'll not fight and we'll have to kill him with his gun in its holster and word will travel far and wide and the D-Ring-T will be called outlaw.

Taper led the way out of the yard at a hard gallop.

In town, Bowdrey sat calmly eating a steak in the Jinglebob Cafe and waited for Grey Taper. He knew the man would come.

Wag Jorstad, a grizzled forty-five-year-old cowman with the stamp of the desert on him, looked up at the tall rider with the leather contraption on his gunhand and said, "Reckon we owe you, stranger. I'm Wag Jorstad, this here's my sister, Amelia," and he nodded toward a tiny woman who looked at him with sharp blue eyes that stood out in startling clarity against her sun-browned face.

"Sorry about the boy," Vent said. "Kin of yourn?"

"My aunt's boy. Rode for us since he was just a pup. Paw killed down in Tucson by a two-card monte dealer. I been kinda raising the boy . . . His maw is shore gonna be tore up."

"Damn that Hazen Branda," one of the men said. Vent glanced at him and noted the sullen mouth, the eyes that never seemed to remain in one place for very long, and the nervous hands and thought mildly, pilgrim.

Nodding at him, Jorstad said, "This here's Butch Hanks and that feller over yonder bringing up the horses is Lud McKiver, my foreman. The dead boy was Jimmie Doolin."

Vent nodded and said, "I'm Vent Torrey from Missouri."

McKiver, a tough forty-year-old rider whose lined face and hard eyes would warn off a knowing man, looked at Vent sharply, then said, "Vent Torrey, huh? Well, well, no wonder them boys of Branda's decided to call it a day."

"You know this feller?" Jorstad asked.

The girl moved away from the dead boy and regarded Vent with quiet curiosity. He had his look and wondered how much money Jorstad spent on her clothes. She was wearing a neat pair of bench-made boots adorned with silver-mounted spurs, a leather split skirt popular in that part of the country because of its durability, a man's checkered shirt, and an almost-new John B. Stetson hat with a curled brim. On her hip was a man-sized .45 in a silver-mounted holster and belt, and Vent figured that if he ever put a price on his horse it would come to just about what three of the conchos were worth.

McKiver had been watching Vent as he examined the diminutive Amelia, as had Hanks, and it was obvious that Hanks didn't like the way the girl was looking at this tall stranger. Got his hat set for the lady, Vent guessed, staring at Hanks and wondering if any western woman in her right mind would trail with such an obvious greenhorn.

Now McKiver said, "I don't know him personally, but I've crossed his reputation a time or two."

Looking at Vent, Jarstad said, "That true? You got a rep?"

Vent carefully rolled a cigarette and, sitting with his knee crooked around the saddle horn, fired it alive with a match from his hat band and nodded. "People talk . . ."

"I reckon they do," McKiver agreed and, turning to Jorstad, said, "This here gent's called Leatherhand, and he's waltzed around the mulberry bush a few times."

The Appy snorted and Vent clucked and walked him to the waterhole. The horse buried his nose in the water and drank for a long time. Finally, he raised his head and blew water and foam and snuffled, then stood waiting for his next command. He did not move.

"That's some horse you got there, mister," Hanks remarked. "You wanna sell him?"

"Not for sale," Vent said shortly and turned the animal back and walked him around in front of the little group. "This feller Branda, what's he do to earn his bread and beans?" he asked.

"More like steak and eggs," Jorstad said. "He runs a two-by-four bustout joint over in Jerome called the Devil's Rondeevoo. Gambling, women, likker. The place has done well. Jerome's a fair-sized city. Lot of mining money floating around there just for the taking. Branda don't mind how he takes."

"How'd you get cross-hitched with him?" Vent asked, wondering why he was interested. In the West of that time and period a man didn't buy into another man's troubles unless he had a stake or was on the man's payroll. Vent had a bigger concern. He knew Grey Taper would be somewhere on his back trail with fifty men and he wouldn't stop until he had Vent on the end of a rope. It was no time to shoulder another man's load.

"Branda wants this waterhole. It's the only watering spot for better than a hundred miles of desert," Jorstad explained.

Hanks, apparently not much interested in all this, had walked off and was now sitting on a boulder smoking and staring hungrily at Amelia Jorstad. McKiver had squatted on his heels and was busily rolling a smoke, his face shaded by his hat brim.

"That's a good enough reason for a man to go to killin' and rampagin' in this country," Vent observed.

Jerking his head toward Amelia, Jorstad added, "And the damn civet cat wants Amelia into the bargain."

Hanks looked up and said harshly, "Well, he ain't gettin' her. He'll have to deal with me first," and he slapped his pistol butt. Vent noted that he wore the gun in an awkward position high on his right hip with the butt forward and wondered who he had learned that from. Whoever it was signed the man's death warrant if he ever came up against a real pistol fighter, Vent figured.

Jorstad ignored Hanks, but when McKiver looked at Vent, the embarrassment was plain to see in his face. Vent winked.

"You own a ranch around here?" Vent asked.

Jerking his head west, Jorstad said, "Yep. Run my stock on two thousand acres over toward Jerome. Ain't worth a damn without this waterhole. Bring my cows over here to these canyons where they's shade and good grass. They come here to water."

"What about the 'Paches?" Vent asked curiously.

"We got us a deal," Jorstad said.

McKiver nodded in agreement. "I know a couple of the young chiefs. Always treated 'em right. When Mr. Jorstad came in here, I went to work for him. Dickered out a deal with the 'Pache. We give them a few cows each year for beef, and they leave the rest alone and even help us make our roundups. Of course, we pay them regular riders' wages."

Vent was amazed. He had never heard of Indians, particularly a wild tribe like the Apache, who hated white men with a hate born of years of mistreatment, working cattle for any man. They usually stole what they wanted, considering it a mark of manhood, and killed any white man who got in their way. Staring down at McKiver, he suddenly had a newfound respect for the man.

"Wag, what we going to do about Jimmie?" Amelia Jorstad asked.

Shaking his head, Jorstad said quietly, "We'll just have to load him up and take him home to his maw."

"What about the waterhole?" Hanks asked in his petulant voice.

"What about it?" Jorstad asked.

"Well, ain't you worried that Branda will come back and dynamite it all to hell and gone?"

Jorstad smiled grimly. "Not hardly. The hole's no good to him unless it's full of water. He figures on building a hotel here for travelers, a sorta big casino and high-falutin' gambling layout where anything goes. He'll charge for the water and clean out the suckers."

Hanks shook his head stubbornly. "He can come in and squat on it as soon as we're gone and that'll be it."

Again Jorstad shook his head. "Can't. The minute he moves in here with me still alive and kicking, I'll have the whole damn United States Cavalry down on him, saber and dragoon pistol."

"I still think somebody ought to hang around here and keep an eye on things," Hanks said, and Vent began to wonder what the man was really after.

"Maybe you're volunteering?" Jorstad asked.

"I'm needed on my place," Hanks said, and it was the first Vent knew the man wasn't working for Jorstad. Now he began to understand McKiver's embarrassment. Hell, nobody liked having a rank tenderfoot as part of anything.

Hanks glanced at Vent, then said casually, too casually, "Why don't we just hire Mr.—is it Torrey?—to guard the well for us? He's pretty good with his gun and he don't seem to mind shooting people."

So that's your game, Vent thought as McKiver suddenly stood up and whirled on Hanks, snarling, "You damn fool. Why don't you put a boot in that big mouth of yours before I close it."

"Easy, Lud," Jorstad counseled.

Amazingly Hanks' hand had dropped to his gun, and suddenly he didn't look anything like a tenderfoot. Instead, he looked like a deadly rattler about to strike. His face had taken on a narrow, closed cast, and his eyes were no longer shallow. Instead, there were no bottoms to them.

McKiver kept his hand away from his gun. Vent, still unconvinced that a man who wore his gun in that position could be very dangerous, smiled bleakly at Hanks and remarked, "You seem all-fired quick to want fight. You want this waterhole so bad you sit on it . . . and when you look at me you either keep your hand off that gun or use it."

For just a few moments, Vent thought Hanks would go for it, and thinking that, said ever so softly, "If you go, friend, you better go damn fast because if you don't you're gonna be history."

Jorstad, alarm showing in his face, stepped between them and started to say something when Vent ordered sharply, "Mr. Jorstad, step away. You know better than that," and Jorstad, range bred and raised, knew Vent was right. You didn't interfere. Reluctantly, he moved off and stood by his sister, who was watching Vent with a strange fascination, as if he were some new and terrible phenomenon come to visit them at this waterhole. He hadn't moved a muscle, yet he seemed to have changed even more radically than had Hanks. It was there to see in the bulge of muscle seen through his gray shirt, in the splayed fingers resting on his chap pocket inches from his gun butt, in the tight wary way his eyes now tunneled onto Hanks.

"Make it or break it," Vent said softly.

Slowly Hanks relaxed, then as swiftly as he had metamorphosed into a man who was more than he seemed, he made the transition back to the blustering tenderfoot he appeared to be when Vent first rode up. Looking at him, Vent observed, "Mister, I think I like you better when you're acting mean."

Jorstad laughed and went to Hanks and slapped him on the back, saying, "Hell, Mr. Torrey, old Butch here, he was just funnin'. He ain't no gunfighter. He came out from the east three years ago and bought a place a little west and north of me."

Hanks looked at the ground, cleared his throat and said, "That's the right of it, Mr. Torrey. I was only playing you. I was an amateur actor back East. Use' to do stage shows and what all. I can change like a flash."

Vent wasn't fooled for one minute. He knew Hanks had been a heartbeat away from testing him but, not sure of who or what Vent was, had decided to wait for another time. "If I was you, I'd be damn careful pullin' that stunt out in this part of the country," Vent warned. "Could get a feller killed plumb dead."

Jorstad, looking relieved that gunplay had been avoided, said, "You're welcome to ride back to the ranch with us, Mr. Torrey. I figure we owe you," and he glanced at Hanks, who looked away.

McKiver sided Vent on the way back to town and, as the horses spaced out for the ride across the valley said, "You believe that stuff about our Mr. Hanks being an actor, and you'll wind up with somebody hitting you in the face with a shovel while you're lyng flat on your back in a hole in the ground."

"What's his story?" Vent asked, looking at McKiver. He wasn't about to forget that the range rider, a tough man with a lot of hard years on his back trail, had avoided trouble with the bogus tenderfoot.

"Right after he rode into Jerome, he got in an argument in a saloon and killed a man with a pretty fair rep of his own. Lot of folks figured it was an accident; that Hanks just got lucky, but I talked to a faro dealer who saw the whole thing; he said Hanks was damn fast, that he pulled and shot before the other feller even cleared leather . . . and he tagged him right dead center through the head at a good twenty-five feet. It wasn't no accident."

Three hours of hard riding put them on the edge of the Verde Valley and within seeing distance of the smoke from the famous Little Daisy Mine and hotel overlooking Oak Creek Canyon.

Jorstad pulled in his horse and pointed off toward a smear of adobe buildings hard against a towering butte on the north end of a wide valley and said, "That's my spread. On further, just to the northwest of me, is Butch's place. His line borders on mine."

Looking at the wide expanse of range Vent wondered how much land Hanks controlled. However you cut it, the two places would make somebody a fine ranch, particularly with the waterhole as part of it, he thought, and figured he had hit on why Hanks resented him.

Worried about me beating his time with the girl, Vent told himself and grinned inwardly.

They rode into the ranch just as the men were coming in from the range and found Jimmie Doolin's mother there. When she saw her son draped over the saddle, she stepped down from the buckboard she had arrived in and walked out and tenderly lifted the boy's head. When she'd had her look, she turned on Jorstad and asked quietly, "What happened, Wag?"

"Branda . . . at the waterhole," was all he said.

Several riders had come from a long adobe bunkhouse near the blacksmith shop, and now they gathered around while two of them helped unload the dead boy and placed him gently in his mother's buckboard.

Jorstad helped her up. Lifting a Winchester across her lap, she said, "I'll go take care of my boy now," and clucked to the team. Seemingly knowing they carried precious cargo, the usually fiesty horses stepped out carefully as the men watched the wagon until it dropped from sight in a depression in the desert.

Jorstad turned to Vent and said, "Damn!" and led the way to the house.

Supper was a solemn affair. Looking across the platter of antelope steaks at Jorstad as he speared a biscuit, Vent read deep hurt in the rancher's eyes. He had obviously been truly fond of the Doolin boy and had taken his death hard. After the meal, the men retired to the wide veranda fronting the sprawling adobe house and, drinks in hand, lighted cigarettes and cigars and settled into wooden chairs scattered along the raised veranda.

"Riders coming," Vent said. He had heard the soft mutter of horses' hooves telegraphing their message on the wind ten minutes earlier, but decided to wait and see if Hanks or Jorstad caught them. McKiver, supper finished, had gone off to the bunkhouse to lay out the following day's work.

Rising, Jorstad moved out to the edge of the veranda and looked south toward Jerome, then said over his shoulder, "Three men. One of 'em looks like Sheriff Ames."

Vent rose in turn, walked to the steps leading into the yard, and stopped there, leaning against a roof support. His face was partially hidden behind a climbing rose vine as the three horsemen rounded into the yard and cakewalked their animals to within twenty feet of the porch.

The lead man wore a star on the front of a dirty vest and sported two guns. He was a big man, but Vent could read weakness and a history of heavy drink in the man's bulbous nose and veined cheeks. He may have once been a good lawman. Now he was what showed through: a man over the hill of life who had become an errand boy for better men.

The man on the sheriff's right was a tall, cadaverous individual with Deep South written all over him. He wore bib overalls and a derby hat, and his feet were encased in a pair of high, flat-heeled boots. One foot dangled free of its stirrup, a careless thing for a man to do who could expect the sudden flair of violence to spook his horse if things went wrong. Looking at him, Vent decided he was only dangerous because of the weapon he carried. Braced against a skinny leg was a heavy, double-barreled shotgun, its bore pointing straight up.

But it was the third man who interested Vent the most. He was a short, chunky Mexican who wore his gun in a shoulder holster on the outside of his shirt, an unusual rig for that era and that part of the country. A serape was drapped across one shoulder, partially concealing the gun, but Vent noted the butt was close to hand. The Mexican rode a beautiful black whose Arabian blood showed clearly in the dished nose and neat body conformation. His feet were adorned with bench-made boots that had to have set the man back a month's salary. On the heels were a pair of long-shanked, silver-mounted spurs partially covered by the bell-bottom trousers he wore. His face was split by a black mustache that swept wide to frame his mouth. A sharp, patrician nose jutted down as if attempting to make contact with a mouth that was filled with gleaming teeth. Those teeth seemed perpetually exposed in a wide grin as the Mexican sat his horse and with one hand pushed the huge, tasseled sombrero back from his forehead.

" 'Lo, Chollo," Vent said quietly and moved away from the porch support.

The Mexican did not lose his smile, but his body suddenly became a still thing and his hands remained on the fancy saddle horn.

Cocking his head to one side he said, "Ah, amigo. *Como 'sta* Leatherhand?"

"Long way from Texas, ain't you?" Vent countered.

"*Sí*, a long way from Texas. Texas, she gets a little bit warm for Chollo, so Chollo come away to thees place."

Pointing a finger at Vent, the sheriff suddenly asked, "You this here feller they call Leatherhand?"

I'm not going to like this gent, Vent told himself, but nodded, not taking his eyes off the Mexican.

"Well, hombre, you're under arrest, so just hand over that gun," the sheriff ordered.

Chollo chuckled as he turned to the sheriff. "Mr. Sheriff, you did not tell me this was the man you wanted. If you had, Chollo would have gone to the cantina instead and ate *frijoles* and *jalapeños* and danced with the *señoritas* . . . So now I think I go do that." He turned his horse and started away.

The sheriff wheeled his horse and rode in front of him, shouting, "Dammit, Chollo, you been sworn in as my deputy. You can't just ride out. We got us here a genuine killer. We gotta take him back to Jerome."

"You should have brought more men," Chollo said.

"Hell, they's three of us," he said, nodding his head toward Jorstad, and added, "Mr. Jorstad there, he's an honest rancher. He won't interfere, will you, Mr. Jorstad?"

Jorstad grinned. "Nope. Won't be any need to. Leatherhand here, he'll just naturally bump you and your two deputies off and we'll have to haul you all the way back to town."

Staring at the rancher, Ames said, "Hell, man, he can't take all three of us . . ."

"I'll take you first, Sheriff . . . if you are sheriff."

"I'm a sheriff and you're gonna damn well find that out, Mr. Gunfighter," Ames blustered.

"Crap," said McKiver, who had drifted up from the bunkhouse carrying a Winchester under his arm.

Turning on him, Ames snarled, "You stay outta this, McKiver, or, by God, I'll see you hanged."

"By the way, what's the charge, Sheriff?" Jorstad asked.

"Murder," the sheriff said triumphantly. "This hombre gunned down a helpless man over by your waterhole. Shot him right smack dab in the gizzard. Killed him as dead as Adam's old ox, he did."

Jorstad stepped off the porch and said, "Sheriff, I was out there and Mr. Torrey here stepped in and kept Hazen Branda and his men from hanging us, including my sister. He killed that feller when the man went for a gun."

"I don't know why you want to go and stick up for this outlaw," Ames whined.

"Since when did Branda buy you off, Ames?" McKiver asked.

"I warned you McKiver. Now, by God, you've gone too far," the sheriff said and reached for his gun.

Vent had never stopped watching Chollo, and now he waited for the Mexican's move. When it came it was fast, but Vent was faster. He shot Chollo right through the chest, and as the Mexican was slammed back over the cantleboard, his horse lunged into the shotgun-wielding southerner's horse, and it leaped wildly straight out from under the man, dropping him flat on his back. The shotgun went off with a roar, sending a full load into his horse's head and killing it instantly.

As the horse dropped like a stone, Ames' hands suddenly shot skyward, and he shouted, "Don't shoot, for God's sake!"

Looking at him with utter disdain, Jorstad walked out, lifted the lawman's gun free, and stepped back, saying, "Just in case you get a sudden seizure of the braveries."

McKiver had relieved the lanky deputy of his shotgun, and now the man was bending over his dead horse cursing in a slow, deadly monotone.

Walking over to him, Jorstad slapped him off his feet and snarled, "They's a lady present. Keep yer mouth closed."

Vent glanced at the porch and saw Amelia standing there staring at him. Walking over to the sheriff, he looked up at the lawman and said softly, "Mr. Sheriff, you're getting too old for this business. Drift out. Try Oregon or California. Lot of opportunities up north. Make any choice you like, but if I see you in this part of the country again, you'll become undertaker bait. *Comprende*, hombre?"

Shakily the sheriff nodded his head and without a word turned his horse and rode north.

Vent went to the southerner, who was still crouched near his horse, and asked coldly, "Where you from?"

"Tennessee," the man answered sullenly.

"I'm from Missouri. Name's Torrey. My family was all Torreys. You understand?"

Staring at Vent wide-eyed the man said, "Yes sir, Mr. Torrey. I understand. What you want fer me ta do?"

Nodding at the dead man, Vent said, "Take that and haul it off and bury it somewhere. Then keep the horse. Use him to go help the sheriff in whatever project he's planning on up north."

Shaking his head, the Tennessean rose and, with McKiver's help, got the dead Mexican draped across the saddle. Before he mounted himself he said, "Mr. Torrey, I never figured they was a man alive who could beat that Mex. He was the fastest thing anybody in Jerome ever saw."

"There's always somebody faster," Vent said and watched the lanky southerner ride north.

Chapter III

"Well, yonder comes Taper an' he's got six men with him," said Carl Shipley, who was standing at the door of the Jinglebob Cafe.

Does he figure it'll take that many? Bowdrey wondered as he mopped up the last of his steak juice with a piece of Shipley's homemade bread.

Shipley moved away from the door and walked back toward his kitchen, then paused and, staring at Bowdrey, said, "No reason why you can't just slip out the back door, Earl."

Bowdrey looked up at the cafe owner and said, "Carl, they's an old rule in this business of marshaling that a man never breaks. No matter what happens, you never run. Once a feller runs, he had just as well keep on running till he gets to the ocean, and then keep right on going, 'cause he's done for anyway."

"They'll kill you, Earl," Shipley said flatly. "You know that, don't you?"

"Probably," the marshal agreed, "but then again, Taper's no fool. He kills me and he outlaws the D-Ring-T. I'm not sure he wants that."

"When a man is dead, they ain't no changing his mind," Shipley remarked and went into the kitchen and closed the door. Bowdrey leaned back in his chair and waited, toothpick jutting from the corner of his wide mouth. As he sat there, the stage came in from the north, its driver howling like a Comanche, whip cracking, as the bulky Wells Fargo Concord rocked past the cafe, headed for the station down street. When the dust had drifted west on a rising desert wind, Bowdrey could see Taper's horses tied at the hitchrack in front of the Red Horse. Fortifying himself, he thought bleakly.

Earl Bowdrey had known Grey Taper since he rode into Dry Springs and had always respected him, even though he was known as a hard man who usually dispensed his own rustler justice and ruled his huge cattle empire with bullwhip and six-shooter. There was one thing the marshal knew about Taper: He fancied himself as a fair man. It was on that fancy Bowdrey was now staking his life.

As he sat calmly waiting, the batwings of the saloon swung wide, and Taper led his men across the dusty street and into the cafe, where they fanned out along the front wall with Taper two paces from the door.

"Earl." Taper nodded, watching the marshal, who had both hands wrapped around a coffee cup.

"Grey," Bowdrey said and, lifting the cup to his mouth, took a long drink and set it back down. His hands had been rock steady, and Taper marveled at the man's iron nerve.

"You know why I'm here, don't you?" Taper asked, his thumbs hooked into his sagging gunbelt. As he stood there seemingly filling half the room with his bulk, Bowdrey looked into his depthless black eyes and wondered inanely if the story that Taper was part Indian was true.

"I know, but I'd best warn you, Grey, that the man

who busts a cap on me outlaws himself and his ranch," Bowdrey said quietly.

"A fair fight is a fair fight," Taper said bleakly. "Let's move out to the street."

Bowdrey looked at him and said distinctly, "No."

"What?" Taper asked, startled.

"I said no," the marshal repeated. Leaning against the wall, Cameron Spencer thought, Now Taper'll kill him and that's the beginning of the end of the D-Ring-T.

"You don't move out to the street, we'll do it right here," Taper warned. He did not like this, but he was a man born with a stubborn streak and that same stubborn streak would not allow him to turn his back on this thing. Silently he cursed his dead son, who had been useless while alive and was now reaching from the land of the dead to tear the D-Ring-T apart and put friend against friend.

"Then do it and be damned," Bowdrey said and stared straight into Taper's eyes and waited.

Taper nodded his head once and said softly, "Kill him, Smiley," and he was still looking into the marshal's eyes when Brown's slugs tore into Bowdrey's chest and drove him back and down in a sprawling heap on the floor.

Slowly and with terrible concentration, Bowdrey managed to get his hands flat under him and lift himself to a sitting position. Turning his head he looked at Taper and said, "Couldn't even stomp your own snakes, Grey Taper . . . getting old . . ."

Taper watched as Bowdrey fell on his side and died.

Spencer turned, walked out the door, and went to his horse and mounted him. He rode to the sidewalk in front of the cafe and looked at Taper, who had just stepped through the front door, and said, "I'll be picking up my gear and my private horse. I'd recommend you give my job to Cole, but that's your choosing." He raised his hand and rode toward the ranch.

Taper stood and watched him ride out of sight, then looked at Cole Butram and said softly, "He always did have a soft streak, but he's the best damn cowman I ever had working for me. I'll take his advice. You're the new ramrod, Cole."

The man in the black gambler's garb had been riding for three days now and had missed being taken by Grey Taper's riders half a dozen times. Those riders were spread out all the way from Dry Springs to the Verde Valley. They were camped at waterholes and mountain passes. Because of this the gambler had had to ride through some of the roughest country in all of Arizona. Now he leaned forward and patted the big black stud's neck and talked softly to him, wishing he had just half a can of oats to feed the big animal.

As he worked his way along a narrow rimrock trail, he glanced down into the spread of desert, with its towering pinnacles of rock stabbing giant fingers into the air as if admonishing God, and thought hell would probably be like this.

Then he spotted the lean line of riders trotting their horses parallel to the rimrock trail. He pulled the stud to a quick stop at a place in the trail where an upthrust boulder gave him cover and looked at the riders carefully.

"Damn," he said softly, and the stud cocked an ear and turned its head slightly as if waiting for a command. The riders, all nine of them, were Apaches. There was no mistaking them. They rode like the wild desert nomads they were, each sitting his animal as if grown there, rifle held against the right thigh, the sun sparkling off the rows of shells stuffed into shoulder-draped bandoleers, bright rags wound around foreheads to hold back dangling black hair.

The gambler wasn't fooled by the fact they seemed to be ignoring him, that they appeared to be bent on an errand of their own. He knew they had spotted him long ago and were now pacing him, playing with him as a cat tosses the mouse away, lets it run, and then pounces again, finally devouring it quick as a flash. He knew that when the Apaches were ready, they would eat him just as the cat eats the mouse.

The trail he rode circled up and onto the broad expanse of the rimrock, where the surface was as flat as a tabletop. Then it dropped down the other side, to end finally in a deep canyon with only one way out. When the gambler had first rode up the trail, he had tied the stud to a rock and clambered to the tabletop flatness of the plateau, walked west until he could peer into the canyon, and saw the trail would lead him down eventually. Now he was halfway around the face of the rim, and below him nine Apaches paced him; and he knew that if he turned back, they would be at the bottom of the trail waiting for him, and if he went on and rode down into the next canyon, he'd find them there too.

"Boxed," he said disgustedly and realized he had been so intent on getting clear of Taper's men that he had overlooked the more dangerous enemy the Apache represented.

Stepping off the horse, he took a long, thin cigar from his black coat and, biting off an end, thrust it between his lips and lighted it with a kitchen match. Leaning against a rock, he sluiced the sweat from his face and decided to wait them out for at least a while.

He figured it had to be over 100 degrees on that trail, and after ten minutes, he removed his coat and tied it behind the cantle. Then he lifted the canteen from the saddle horn, wet his handkerchief, and let the horse suck up the moisture. He had his own brief taste of the water, then capped the canteen and returned it, making certain the strap was fastened tightly to the horn. For a man to lose a canteen out here was to sign his own death warrant, he knew, then thought ruefully, Hell, that's my death warrant riding down there, as he watched the Apaches suddenly pull in and ride beneath the rimrock overhang. Looking for shade, he thought and led his own horse along the trail.

He continued to walk until he came out on top of the plateau. Mounting, he rode across its flatness and, reaching the trail on the other side, started down. There was no indication the Apaches had circled the end of the towering rimrock yet, but he figured they were probably down there waiting for him. He had made his decision to ride on down and if they came at him, make a stand. He didn't give himself much room for hope but was determined to take out as many as he could.

Halfway down the trail he saw a swift movement at the mouth of the canyon as one of the Indians ran from one side of the narrow opening to the other in search of a better ambush. Reaching behind the saddle, he unsheathed his rifle, levered a shell into the chamber and rested it across his thighs. Then he lifted the heavy .45 from holster and carefully checked the action out of habit more than anything else. He knew it was in perfect working order, but years of living by the weapon had taught him to make his survey before committing himself to war. Satisfied, he dug out another cigar and lit up. Puffing smoke as if nothing were happening, he rode on out on the floor of the canyon; then, at the last minute, and not really knowing why he was doing it, he turned up canyon and rode around a bend. Once out of sight of the Indians, he put the horse to a run and swung him from bend to bend, looking over his shoulder for pursuit. When the canyon ran out, he pulled the stud in on it haunches and left the saddle on the jump, knowing they had to be breathing down his neck.

At the end of the canyon a towering rock wall thrust straight up for three-hundred feet. At its base a pile of boulders, apparently having fallen from above, furnished the cover he had been looking for, and he led the horse far back among the rocks, seeking a safe place for him.

Even if he won this fight, but was left afoot, he would still be as dead as if one of the Apaches had lifted his hair. Tying the horse securely, he dug two boxes of shells from his saddlebags and walked back to take up a stand behind a narrow boulder that afforded him a clear view of the lower canyon, yet furnished adequate cover.

Carefully piling a handful of rifle cartridges in a shallow depression in the rock, he checked to make sure the Winchester was fully loaded, then spread out half a box of .45s in another hollow. The rest of the rifle shells went in his right-hand pocket and the .45s in his left.

He was ready. He waited, hat cocked over his eyes. He had calculated the odds as any good gambler should and had found them not to his liking, but knew he was in a game in which cashing out meant dying. It was the biggest game of all, a game he had played more than once in his life. He had always won. Now he wasn't so sure of the outcome.

The first shot came from an overhang two-hundred feet down canyon. He saw movement a second before the Apache fired, and ducked, then answered the shot, cursing softly when his bullet whined away harmlessly after ploughing into the rock a foot from the Indian's head.

That first shot was followed by a flurry of them, and all the gambler could do was hunker down and weather them as they struck the cliff behind him and droned viciously into his hiding place, smashing rock chips into his face and knocking a chunk from one boot heel.

When the last shot died away, he looked up quickly, saw an Indian sprinting toward a rock nearer to his position, and fired a wing shot that went dead true, taking the running Apache through the upper chest and piling him dead in the sand. Sharp watched the man's death throes as he jerked spasmodically then subsided, seeming to shrink before the gambler's eyes.

Loud shouts followed his lucky hit, and more shots poured more lead into his position. When the firing ceased, he was amazed to discover he was still untouched. Cards must be running my way, he thought. His canteen lay between two rocks, and he lifted it now, had his token sip, and replaced it. Slightly refreshed, he looked out carefully. A hundred feet from his position there was a narrow slit in the canyon wall that he had noticed when he galloped into this cul-de-sac. Now he saw a shadow cast on the down-canyon side of the cut and guessed, One of the buggers is hid in there. Lifting his rifle, he sighted it on the shadow and fired three rapid shots.

The bullets struck the rock and bounced back into the up-canyon side of the cut. A sharp cry answered this venture, then an Apache, his face smeared with blood, staggered into the open canyon. The gambler ruthlessly cut him down and was instantly besieged again as the Apaches poured shot after shot into his position. When they quit firing again he relaxed. A faint trickling sound at his feet brought him instantly back to attention as he looked toward his boots, where his canteen was gushing forth the last of its contents into the desert sands. A bullet had apparently ricocheted into it, tearing a gaping hole. Snatching it up, he managed to gulp down a cupful before it ran dry.

Holding it in his hand, he thought bleakly, now they've got me. All they have to do is wait, and Apaches were famed for their patience. They had been known to crouch at a waterhole for forty-eight hours, totally motionless, waiting for a deer, then kill it with one well-placed shot. They would do the same for him, he knew. When he was forced out by the driving need for water, they would kill him.

He had killed two. Seven still waited out there. As he hunkered in his refuge he thought, funny thing here, I always figured somebody would beat me to the draw over a card table. This, he told himself, is no way for any man to die.

As the long day crawled by, he daydreamed of water and the cool interior of saloons he had worked in until finally, just as the sun began its day's-end run down the slope of the world, he decided to go out with dignity instead of hiding in the rocks like some animal until he went mad or blew his own brains out. Stuffing the shells into his pockets he slipped away to where the stud waited, and leading him back to the entrance to his barricade, he stroked the big animal's neck, saying softly, "Well, old pal, if I draw a bad hand out there, I reckon you'll get picked up in the pot," and stepped into the saddle. Pulling his hat down, he slipped the long gun into its scabbard, palmed his .45, and, slamming the gigs to the black, burst from cover at a dead run. He made the corner before the Apaches realized what he was doing, and as a consequence he caught three of them squatting in the middle of the canyon floor holding a powwow. Lifting the .45, he fired three times and was rewarded by three tumbling bodies.

As he whirled to seek another target, a pistol boomed

from just around the bend, then boomed twice more. As the gambler sat his horse and stared, an Apache came around the bend backward, his rifle at his hip and firing down canyon. The gambler lifted his gun and shot the Indian in the back. As he dropped, a sudden stillness fell over the canyon. The gambler calmed the stud, looked around at the sprawled bodies then fired up another cigar and, gun held loosely at his side, waited.

He heard the horse before he saw the rider. Then a tall man wearing a gray hat and riding a magnificent Appaloosa came cakewalking the animal around the bend, a rifle across the swells and his eyes carefully cataloging all he saw. Riding up to the man in black, he said, "Got another one of them cigars, Owney?"

Smiling, Owney Sharp dug out his last cigar and handed it over. "Leatherhand, nice to see you."

"I count nine dead. That all of them?"

Sharp nodded his head.

Dismounting, Vent went to each body and stripped away the belts and removed three handguns worn by the three killed out in the middle of the canyon when Sharp burst from cover and caught them cold. Two of the rifles were Sharps, one was an old cavalry weapon, a Springfield, and the rest were lever action weapons, including a heavy .45-90.

Looking at Sharp, Vent asked, "You want the rifles or pistols?"

"Pistols will be fine," Sharp answered and went and gathered up the three Colt .45s. He figured the Apaches had probably lifted them from the bodies of an unfortunate patrol they had surprised somewhere in the lonely reaches of the desert.

Slinging the gunbelts from his saddle horn, the gambler said, "You sorta popped up at the right time there . . ."

"Got a camp just over in the next canyon. Heard the shots and figured by the sounds it was one man against several. Decided to even the odds."

"You know these canyons are crawling with Taper's men," Sharp asked. It was a statement rather than a question.

Vent nodded as he mounted the Appaloosa. "I know. Seen half a dozen over toward the Fort Winslow stage road and another eight or ten up on the Little Colorado."

Sharp stepped aboard the stud and reined him in alongside Vent. As they moved down canyon, he said, "Much obliged for the put-in. Reckon I'd be a memory by now if you hadn't come along."

"Hell, looked to me if you was doing right smart there," Vent grinned. "How'd ya catch them three out in the open that way?"

"Decided to make a ride for it. Go out with a howl instead of a sniffle. Play the whole wad on a last hand. Came busting outta that pile of rocks and caught them flat-footed right there in the middle of the wash."

"The hell. What ya reckon they was doin?"

"Probably shaking the sticks to see who got my rifle and pistol and who got old Blackie here," Sharp said with a slight grin.

"What brings you way ta hell and gone over here?" Vent asked curiously.

"Runnin' from the same bunch you are. Taper's crowd."

Vent looked at him sharply. "What's Taper's argument with you?"

"I had a difference of opinion with three of his riders in the Red Horse," Sharp said. "When the game was over, I had all the cards and them fellers had drawn the black aces."

As they rounded from the canyon and rode west, Vent

said somberly, "Met a gent passing through two days ago. He said he was on the stage at Dry Springs when Taper rode in with six men. They went into the Jinglebob and Smiley Brown shot Bowdrey dead. Earl never even drew his gun . . . Hell of a note."

"You worked with Bowdrey one time, didn't you?"

Vent nodded. "We was marshals up at Cripple Creek for a few months. As good a man as ever pinned on a star. Taper's got some answering to do."

Sharp glanced at the tall man riding beside him, and the look on Vent Torrey's face made him very happy he wasn't working for Taper. "He was my friend too," Sharp said, then asked, "Cam Spencer have anything to do with that?"

Vent shook his head. "No, Spencer rode out to the ranch and picked up his gear and pulled his freight. Up and quit the old man flat. Told folks in Dry Springs before he left that he wasn't about to work for an outfit that had turned outlaw. Cole Butram's now the new wagon boss of the D-Ring-T."

As they rode into the next canyon, Sharp asked curiously, "How you gonna handle this thing, Torrey? You can't fight fifty men."

"Hell, I don't want to fight any of them, Owney," Vent said and knew deep down that he should just ride on out of Arizona, but also knew that to run would put him in more jeopardy than if he stayed and fought the whole D-Ring-T outfit single-handed. A bunch quitter whose gun is his life is as good as dead. Vent knew.

"Neither do I, but it looks like that's the way of it," Sharp said as they rounded a bend in the canyon and came to a thick grove of trees. Riding into them, Sharp was surprised to see a small spring trickling from a crack in the base of a cliff, its cool waters spreading out from a small pond to turn the grass beneath the trees a rich green.

"How the hell did you ever find this spot?" Sharp asked.

Dismounting and pulling off the saddle, Vent dropped it near a tree and unsheathed his rifle, carrying it to a small camp he had set up between two large boulders. "Feller I met who spends a lot of time up here with the 'Paches told me about it. Says they don't use it anymore unless they go on the warpath. He probably knew that bunch you tangled with, but wouldn't mean much to him. Says these 'Paches go off on the warpath all the time. A stranger they'll kill quick as a cat can wink its eye, but they make a friend and he's a friend for life."

Sharp removed his saddle and carried it over near the bed of coals. Dropping it by a tree, he sat down on it and asked, "That water good?"

Scooping up a tin cupful, Vent handed it to the gambler and urged, "Try it. Cold as if it came from an ice field."

The two men talked until midnight, then sought their bedrolls and sleep.

Vent awoke knowing someone was in the camp. He did not open his eyes. Instead, he arced a thumb over the hammer of his .44, where it lay against his leg and had lain during the night, and continued to breathe normally until he placed the interloper. The soft splash of water told him whoever it was, was sitting under a tree at the edge of the camp. Carefully Vent let his eyes open just a crack. He could make out the shape of a stranger squatting on his heels about ten feet from the end of his bedroll. Both the man's hands were holding a canteen, which he was in the process of drinking from.

Vent opened his eyes the rest of the way and slid the

barrel out from under the blankets, cocked the weapon, and said softly, "'Lo, Cam."

Cam Spencer turned his head and nodded. "Howdy, Leatherhand, how're you?"

"Still alive."

Sharp lifted his gun free and stood up, looked at Cam, and said, "You're a noisy bugger. You damned near stepped on me when you went after that water."

"I reckon I was pretty thirsty. Ran out two days ago."

Vent looked at him sharply. For a man to go without water two days in that blazing inferno of hell and still be able to move around was little short of a miracle.

"Where's your horse?" Sharp asked, looking down canyon.

"Dead. Dropped over on me yesterday."

Vent nodded. "You track us in here?"

"Yep. Saw where you had the dustup with the warwhoops. Tried to locate one of their horses, but guess they done split the wind."

"They ran west of here when I killed the handler," Vent said. "We'll see if we can find them after breakfast."

Spencer stared at the can of peaches Vent was about to open with his Bowie knife, and seeing the barely concealed hunger in the ex-ramrod's eyes, Vent tossed him the can. Then he flipped the Bowie end over end and buried it in the trunk of a nearby tree, saying, "Here, why don't you start on this. While you're getting outside those peaches, I'll get some biscuits and bacon going here." He began building up the fire, deliberately turning his back on Spencer, who was so hungry his hands were shaking almost too much for him to get the can open.

Not wanting to embarrass the man, Sharp went and watered the horses, then restaked them to another patch of grass.

Coming back, Sharp squatted down near Spencer and watched him wolf down the peaches then gulp the juice. "Looks like you went a few days without tying on the feedbag."

Spencer set the can to one side and glanced at Vent, saw he was ready to slice the bacon, and threw the knife, sticking it neatly in the base of a small tree a foot from Vent's knee. "Yeah, I was some that," Spencer said. "Ran out of grub and was afraid to shoot at anything for fear it would bring either the 'Paches or Taper's men."

"You think they got orders to lay you by the boot heels too?" Spencer asked.

"Never know about that old boy. He might just decide I was a traitor to the brand and order my neck stretched. A thing like that would sure enough upset the hell outta my poor old mother."

"To say nothing of your ability to keep on swallowing," Vent observed.

"There is that too," Spencer agreed.

"Looks sorta like we're three fellers in the same corral," the gambler mused as he went to the coffeepot and poured two steaming cups, handing one to Spencer.

"Any ideas?" Spencer asked, glancing at Vent. Whether he was willing to admit it, he was awestruck by this tall, gray-eyed man with the quiet, quick ways of moving and fearsome reputation. Men all over the West knew the name Leatherhand. His shootouts were talked about around roundup campfires, in saloons, and wherever men gathered to discuss such things. Those who had actually witnessed his uncanny speed swore no man alive could best him. There were standing bets between high-stakes gamblers on the results of a shootout between Vent and such men as James Butler Hickok, known on the frontier as Wild Bill, John Wesley Hardin, Wyatt Earp, or the murderous Doc Holliday, him of the cold gray eyes and the savage temper, who was quarrelsome to a fault and killed at the drop of an insult. The relative speeds of these men and more were often discussed, and always the name Leatherhand came up.

Leatherhand himself sometimes wondered what would happen if he met one of these men. He had killed his share of fast guns, men like the Mexican, Chollo, but they were local pistol fighters only, and known by few, where the names of men like Holliday were known and repeated all over the West.

Now Vent tossed a handful of bacon slices into the iron skillet, took the lid off the Dutch oven, looked in at the biscuits just turning brown and crisp, and poured himself a cup of coffee. Then he addressed Spencer's question.

"I figure old man Taper sent most of his boys out gallivantin' all over this part of Arizona looking for me, so why not just go where he ain't," he said, staring at them over his cup rim.

"That might not be a bad idea, but where would that be? Hell, his men are everywhere," Sharp said.

Thinking about Branda and Jorstad for a moment, the face of Butch Hanks floated into his mind's eye and he asked the gambler, "You ever run into a feller name of Butch Hanks, a kind of tenderfoot type that ain't really a tenderfoot?"

Sharp smiled. "So you met old Butch, huh? Yeah, I know him. He's a flimflam man from way back. Usually when he's around you gotta lock up the ladies and bury yore money in the post-hole bank."

"Good with a gun, is he?" Vent asked, dishing up the bacon and biscuits.

While Spencer fell to, Sharp thought on the question, then said, "I never saw him break leather, but a feller down Santa Fe way told me he thought Hanks could probably pull with the best of them. Said he saw him plug two fellers in a barroom brawl there a year ago, and neither one of 'em got off a shot . . . 'Course they coulda been slow as a dung beetle too."

Between mouthfuls Spencer said, "Seems to me I heard about that gent myself. It was up around Goldfield, Nevada. He was in the army. Salted a claim and got caught at it. Killed a man and left town on a high old lope. They was also something about a young girl. Can't rightly recall, but it was an ugly story. If he's the same man, then he's a bad one to cross."

Vent washed the dishes and saddled his horse, then cleaned up the camp, putting out the fire and burying the partially burned pieces of wood in the sand. While he worked, Sharp removed all evidence of boot tracks from the sandy areas leading to the spring, filled all the canteens, and, saddling his black, mounted and pulled his boot from the stirrup so that Spencer could get on behind him.

Mounting, Vent said quietly, "Why don't we drop into Jerome and visit the Devil's Rondeevoo and buck the tiger," and he led them down canyon. An hour later, they caught one of the Indian ponies and Spencer was horseback again.

Half a days' hard ride put them on the Jerome stage road, and as they paced their tired animals, Vent suddenly turned his head, listened carefully for a moment, then told the others, "Riders coming," and swung off the road and behind a large boulder. Spencer and Sharp followed.

As they gazed northward, a bubble of dust moving toward them obliterated the road, and came on, its center filled with running horses. When the wave of dust reached them, Vent recognized McKiver and Amelia and several of the Jorstad ranch hands and rode from cover, sitting his horse by the side of the road.

McKiver slammed his stocky dun to a sliding stop as the other riders followed suit. Rounding on Vent, he said, "Branda tried to bushwack Wag. Damn him to hell, he shot at him from cover. Wag's lucky to be alive."

"Where you goin?" Vent asked, looking at the heavily armed party.

"To town," McKiver said savagely. "Figure on hanging me a back-shooter from his own saloon porch."

Removing his hat, Vent looked at Amelia Jorstad and said, "Nice day for a ride, ma'am. Might be you're heading into something you won't come out of."

Lifting her chin she said, "Wag was almost killed. Somebody's going to pay. We figure it had to be Branda. He started this mess. He's the one who wants our waterhole."

Rolling a cigarette while the Jorstad riders waited patiently, Vent lit up and, glancing off toward the mountains to the east, said softly, "If he did do it, or had it done, he'll be expecting you. He'll have the street lined with guns. You'll never even reach the place."

As they stared at him, he let his eyes roam along the line of riders, then asked, "Where's Hanks?"

"Home, I reckon," McKiver said, but Vent detected a slight note of doubt in the foreman's voice.

"Well, it ain't important," Vent decided. "Why don't we sorta ride in together, and when we reach the edge of town, you folks just kinda lay back and let me and my friends here amble on in, sorta look over the lay of things."

"Ain't your fight," McKiver said stubbornly. "Besides, you done enough helping us out when Branda had us pinned down at the waterhole."

Amelia's voice had softened when she added, "Our

debt to you is almost too large to pay now. Wag has always said a person should stomp his own snakes and not expect others to help him, or do it for him."

"I got me a little side problem with Mr. Branda," Vent said. "I'd kinda like to settle it first. When I get done, you can have what's left." His voice was as cold as an Alaska winter.

McKiver suddenly nodded. "So, that'll be the way of it. We'll wait, but if you ain't outta that hornet's nest in two hours, we come in and pick up the remains and give you some side riders to hell," and he added, "let's ride on."

Long before they reached Jerome, they could see it clinging to the side of Cleopatra Hill surrounded by oak and pine. As they gazed at this modern town in the desolate wastes of the Arizona cliff country, smoke poured from the stacks of smelters. It was a town built by copper, silver and gold, but mostly copper.

As they drew near, Vent marveled at the three-story brick building seemingly clinging by sheer stubbornness to the face of the hillside. The streets were paved with cobblestones, and many of the town's most imposing buildings were constructed of brick.

Pulling their horses up at the bottom of the grade in a small grove of trees, they dismounted, loosened their saddle girths, and watched as Vent and his two side riders went on up the vicious series of switchbacks leading to the town proper.

Rounding into the main street, Vent looked northwest and marked the long rimrock cliffs of Oak Creek Canyon above Verde Valley. As he rode along the street, he did not know it, but before this town smelted the last bar of copper and burned the last chunk of oak cut from the slopes above town the hard rock miners would dig eighty miles of tunnel beneath the streets and haul out $800 million in ore.

They passed an imposing building that Sharp said was a hospital and another brick structure that was clearly marked JAIL. They rode past the offices of the United Verde Mine owned and operated by Sen. William A. Clark, U.S. ambassador to Great Britain. Just before they turned down a long street crowded with saloons, the sidewalks full of miners, they passed an office with a sign over the door creaking in the desert breeze. It said this was the home of the Little Daisy Mine.

Nodding his head at the office, Sharp said, "That's owned by Rawhide Jimmy Douglas. Feller's a Midas. Everything he touches turns to money. They say he's pulling a fortune outta the Little Daisy."

Spencer pointed toward the top of a small knob that thrust out from the main hillside and said, "Boot hill's up thataway."

Vent glanced toward the cemetery and noted the numerous new stone markers and wooden crosses and thought, a place that has its man for breakfast.

They spotted the Devil's Rondeevoo halfway down the block, and Vent wheeled his horse into a hitchrack two doors away and said, "Let's tie on the feedbag. Hate this kind of work on an empty stomach."

They tramped into the first cafe they saw and took a table near the back of the room, looking over the mass of roughly dressed miners, cowboys, ranchers, saloon swampers, and bartenders. At one table, several ladies of the night were voraciously attacking steaks and a huge platter of eggs. At another, several men dressed in suits ate quietly, generally ignoring the crowd. Many of the men present were armed, and those that didn't display a gun probably had one stuck behind a belt or down a boot.

When the waiter came, they ordered the cowboy's special: steak and eggs with a platter of fried potatoes and a pot of black coffee.

While they waited for their order, Vent kept his eyes on the street through the wide front door. There was no screening; flies flew in and out, and an occasional wasp droned in and took roost somewhere in the rafters. Then he saw Smiley Brown. He remembered the bandy-legged little gunman from the days at Dry Springs when he rode to town with Bert Taper to tie one on. A lot of the men around the little cow town were afraid of his reputation, but Vent figured him a horse with no bottom.

"What kinda gent is Smiley Brown?" he asked Spencer.

"Rattler without the rattles," Spencer said immediately. "He's living on a rep that some of us figured he made up himself."

"Ever hear of anybody trying him?" Vent asked as the waiter set their steak and eggs on the table and followed them with a huge pot of coffee on a wooden block burned black by hundreds of such pots.

"Nope," Spencer said and dished up a huge pile of fried potatoes onto his plate, noting, "I don't reckon I'll ever get full again."

"Smiley just went into Branda's place," Vent said quietly, and Spencer stopped eating and looked up, mouth full, to stare at the big gunfighter.

"The hell you say?" he said softly.

Sharp brushed a spot of dust from his sleeve and glanced out the door. "They's a couple more of Taper's hands across the street," he said.

"Would they know your horse?" Vent asked Sharp.

"Spot him in a minute," Sharp said.

Calmly finishing their meal, the men rose, left money on the table, and, walking to the back of the room, let themselves into an alley. They followed it until they came to a corner and stepped into the street. Vent had his careful look at doorways and rooftops, then led the others west until he reached the street where they had left their horses.

Looking around the corner, Spencer said, "Those boys are staked out on our horses."

Vent had his look, and when a roughly dressed miner came by and bumped into him, he looked at the man, who started to say something, then caught Leatherhand's eyes and mumbled an apology and hurried away.

"An alleyway comes into that street just to the right of where they're standing," Vent said and led the way boldly across the intersection, mingling with half a dozen men who were heading for a saloon on the corner. Passing around behind it, they walked along until they reached the cross alley, then turned back and stopped just off the street.

There was nobody near the entrance to the cafe and no one on its roof, so Vent figured these men had been left here merely to report if they returned to their horses. Casually stepping around the corner, he moved up beside the two men. When they glanced around, he said, "Nice day to die," and watched as their eyes widened.

"Who the hell are you?" the taller of the two said sullenly.

"I'm the feller who's gonna down you if you don't step into this alley with me," Vent warned.

The second man came around beside his partner and asked sharply, "What is this, a holdup?"

"You ain't got anything I want except your life," Vent told him bleakly and dropped his hand to his gun butt.

"Hey, ease up there," the tall one said.

His partner grabbed his arm and said, "Better do as

the man says, Ike. He'll down us both. I've heard about this jasper."

They walked quietly around the corner and down the alley, showing surprise when they saw Spencer and Sharp. "Birds of a feather," one of the men said.

Spencer grinned and remarked, "Yeah, ain't it the truth."

Across the street at the cafe, a man sitting near the window rose with a puzzled look on his face, paid his bill, and stepped out onto the street. Reaching into his shirt pocket he extracted a cigar, and as his coat swung back, the sun caught the glitter of the marshal's star he wore on his gunbelt and set a shaft of reflected light dancing across the front of the Devil's Rondeevoo. Biting off the end of the Havana and tucking it into the corner of his mouth, the lawman said half-aloud, "Now I'd a swore that was old Leatherhand just sashayed down that alley," and moved off to follow the five men.

Vent herded his captives around behind the Devil's Rondeevoo, then halted them near the back door, where a small shed housed two saddle horses. Walking inside, he untied a rope from the horn of a saddle hanging from a ceiling beam, then stuck his head back outside and said, "Bring them boys in here." When everybody was inside, he closed the door and proceeded to tie the two Taper men together.

The one called Ike began cursing in a monotone until Vent cuffed him and said mildly, "Quit that," and then finished the job, leaving the men facedown in the straw, their own neckerchiefs stuffed in their mouths.

"Now let's us take a look at the Devil's Rondeevoo," Vent said and led Sharp and Spencer across the alley and through the back door of the gambling joint and tavern.

Inside they found themselves in a narrow hallway

leading toward the front of the building, and they catfooted along it until they reached a second door.

"Sounds like somebody's playing billy-be-damned out of a fiddle," Spencer observed as Vent slowly opened the door and slid inside the barroom, followed by his two companions. The room before them was about sixty feet long and twenty-five feet wide. On one side a mahogany bar reflected in a full-length backbar mirror was lined with patrons. A dozen tables along the opposite wall were being used for keno, three-card monte, and poker games. Near the front of the room couples sat and tapped their toes to a rousing tune being played on a fiddle by a cadaverous black man wearing bib overalls. He was barefoot. On his head he wore a crushed felt hat tied beneath his chin with a piece of dirty cord. Between his huge bare feet a tin cup was half-full of coins, attesting to the appreciation of the music lovers in the place.

Vent glanced toward the end of the bar and saw the cold hard eyes of the gunman Von O'Brien fixed on him. "Spotted," he said out of the corner of his mouth.

"Which one?" Sharp asked.

"Gent in black. Name of O'Brien. Fancies himself a hand with a sidearm," Vent said, keeping his eyes on the man in the black chaps.

"Heard of him," Sharp said, and then Branda came through a back door and walked down the plank, stopping beside two men. One was Smiley Brown. The two men shook hands and began a quiet conversation as O'Brien, alarm showing on his face, hurried down the bar toward Branda and Brown.

"Who's the gent with Brown?" Vent asked Spencer.

"Tiny Hayden. Big head with nothing in it but sawdust. As slow in his head as a deadbeat paying off a gambling debt. No worry."

Vent suddenly dropped his hand to his gun and, looking directly at O'Brien, shook his head. The man stopped as if he had run into a wall. Then he turned slowly, said something to the man behind him, and, when the man quickly moved away, placed his back to the bar.

His lips in a half smile, Vent nodded at O'Brien, then turned to watch Branda and Brown. While he had been involved in the byplay with O'Brien, another man had joined Branda, and when Vent recognized him he gave himself a mental pat on the back. The fourth man was Butch Hanks.

Chapter IV

Smoke drifted through the bar. The low rumble of men's voices was a steady monotone against the backdrop of the polished mahogany plank, the walrus-mustached bartender with his white shirt, sleeve-garters, and bow tie, and the glittering array of bottles on the backbar.

Vent and his two companions stood quietly behind a line of drinkers who were watching the antics of the Negro fiddle player and the dancing couples who cavorted in nothing faintly resembling a dance step.

Hanks was leaning toward Branda, talking hurriedly and occasionally glancing toward the front door, where men continued coming and going at a rate that fanned the batwings constantly.

Then Sharp leaned forward and said quietly, "Up in the corner. The balcony," and Vent glanced up to where a tiny balcony hung from the corner of the ceiling. It was occupied by a man toting a sawed-off, ten-gauge shotgun. He had apparently come onto the narrow platform with its heavy railing from a door directly to the rear of where he now sat leaning against the wall, the deadly Greener lying across his thighs, eyes lazily tacking over the room below.

"Time to go," Vent said and led Spencer and Sharp

back through the door, his head half-turned so he could watch O'Brien. When they reached the doorway, Vent stepped through fast, closed the door, and immediately opened a door to their right. Followed closely by his companions, he ducked inside just as a shout went up in the bar, followed by the thunderous roar of the shotgun and a splintering crash from the vicinity of the hallway they had just left.

"Jesus!" Spencer said reverently as the screaming whine of rampant buckshot ripped into the walls and alleyway behind the saloon.

"Lock that door." Vent looked around and, noting a huge desk and a number of filing cabinets and several chairs, figured they had walked into Branda's office.

While Spencer stood by the door, Colt in hand, Sharp leaned against a small bar in the corner, his hand dangling limply near his holstered .45. Vent sat on the edge of the desk watching the door, the butt of his heavy .44 jutting handily.

As they waited, they heard the tramp of running feet then the sharp slam of the outer door as several men passed down the hallway and out into the alley.

Somebody shouted, "Check the stable," and two minutes later a man called out, "Hey, they's a couple of fellers tied up in here."

Spencer's lips peeled back from his teeth in a humorless grin.

Sharp casually poured a drink for each of them, carried one to Spencer, who immediately downed it, and another to Vent. Returning to the portable bar, he lifted his glass and said calmly, "To a fast horse and a gun that never misfires," and tossed the liquor down his gullet.

Vent let his sit while he cocked an ear to the sounds coming from outside. He heard men returning back down the hall, and someone said loudly, "I get a shot at them waddies and, by God, they're dead," and finally it was quiet, with only the soft sound of muffled voices coming from the bar.

"Reckon we better drift?" Spencer asked.

Then someone tried the door and found it locked, and they heard the fumbling sound of a key being slipped into the keyhole. Spencer stepped behind the door and, gun in hand, waited, a slight smile on his face. Vent and Sharp remained where they were.

The door swung open and Branda and O'Brien entered, closed the door and locked it, then turned and stopped, hands dropping to gun butts.

Spencer cocked his Colt.

Turning his head very slowly, O'Brien found himself gazing down the barrel of the heavy weapon and asked, "Now, who the hell are you?"

Spencer grinned. "Just a feller passing through."

Looking at Sharp, O'Brien slowly moved his hands out from his body and said softly, " 'Lo there, gambling man. Long ways from your stomping grounds, ain't you?"

"Where I hang my hat," Sharp said and poured himself a drink.

"You know this gent?" Branda asked, staring at Sharp from a pair of hot eyes, his red mustache fairly bristling.

"I know him. Name's Owney Sharp. Honest gambler. One of the few men around I wouldn't want to match guns with."

"That good, huh?" Branda asked.

"That good," O'Brien said.

Cocking a thumb at Vent, Branda asked, "As good as this hombre is supposed to be?"

"Chollo's dead, ain't he?" O'Brien retorted.

"There is that," Branda agreed.

"Best drop the gunbelts," Spencer advised.

"I'd sorta do it," O'Brien advised and, suiting action to words, unbuckled and let his gunbelt slide to the floor.

"Probably should kinda push it over this way," Spencer said mildly and watched O'Brien comply.

Shrugging, Branda followed suit, but it was obvious he didn't like it.

Vent lifted his glass and drained off the whiskey, then said conversationally, "The only reason you fellers ain't communing with the man at the big gate is because I need a few answers," and he rose and walked across the room, and in each step there was a deadly kind of menace that Branda and O'Brien felt, but did not understand.

Looking uncomfortable, O'Brien, who was no coward, took a backward step as Vent approached him and said, "Hey now . . ."

Vent drew and slammed the .44 alongside O'Brien's head, and the man folded and dropped as if he had been poleaxed. The movement was so swift that none of the men in the room saw it until they heard the sharp crack of the barrel striking bone. O'Brien sighed softly and rolled onto his back and lay still.

Staring down at his hired gunman, Branda said, "Now, that was a hell of a thing to do to a man."

Turning without a word, Vent started across the room toward the bar owner, who backed up until his legs struck the desk, then held up his hands, palms outward, and asked shakily, "What the hell do you want outta me?"

"What was Hanks doing talking to you?" Vent asked as he slid the .44 back in its half-breed holster. Looking into the lean Missourian's eyes, Branda had no doubt this man would kill him and feel about as much emotion as he might generate for a rabid dog.

"He offered me a deal," Branda said. "He offered to deliver the Jorstad place if I'd make him a full partner."

"Nice feller," Sharp observed.

"Did he happen to explain to you just how he planned to get that little chore done?" Vent asked, casually rolling a cigarette.

"Said he was about to go into double harness with the Jorstad girl and that once he had her all roped and tied, he'd make sure old Wag fell off his horse or somethin'."

"I'll bet you just loved that idea," Sharp said.

"I turned him down," Branda replied. "Not because I didn't like it, but because I figure a feller who'd betray his girlfriend's daddy wouldn't hesitate one damn minute to run a sandy on me."

Spencer grinned. "Yeah, since you ain't even wearing a skirt."

O'Brien groaned. Glancing down at him, Branda said, "He'll kill you, you know."

"No, I don't reckon he'll even try. Too smart. Your man there's probably got more brains than you have. He'll figure he's lucky he ain't dead." Vent walked to the door and unlocked it, turned and nodded to Branda, and said, "Thanks for the likker," and stepped into the hall, his hand on his gun.

Sharp stepped clear of Branda, then suddenly drew and hit him behind the ear and watched him drop beside O'Brien, roll over and try to get up, then relax with a sigh into unconsciousness.

Leaving by the alley door, they moved toward the street where they had left their horses, Vent in the lead. Just as they stepped out on the sidewalk, a voice from a recessed doorway behind them said, "Your horses are down at the jail, gents," and Vent turned slowly, then smiled at the husky man standing there with the shotgun cradled under his arm.

"Howdy, Boots, how you?" Vent asked.

"Fine as cat's fur," Boots Thomas said.

Vent, noticing the badge on his gunbelt, nodded and observed, "It figures. Marshal, huh?"

"Yep, marshal," Boots replied and, turning, led the way back along the cross alley, then south two blocks, then east along a cross street one block beyond the Devil's Rondeevoo. Turning north again, the lawman led the trio to the back door of his office and stepped inside. A lanky man wearing a deputy marshal's badge rose and stared at the group, then said softly, "Everything all right, Mr. Thomas?"

"Fine, Del. Just fine," Thomas said as Vent turned to his companions and made introductions.

"This here's Boots Thomas. I marshaled under him at Leadville some years back." Nodding at Spencer and Sharp, Vent said, "Dark clothes here is Owney Sharp from over to Dry Springs. Other gent's Cam Spencer."

Thomas went to a big oak desk and rummaged in a drawer, came up with a bottle, and passed it around. Vent declined. Looking closely at Sharp, the marshal said, "I know you from somewhere . . ."

"I played a few games around Leadville when you was marshal," Sharp said noncommittally.

"Remember now. You killed that tinhorn cheat in Pop Wymon's two-by-four bustout joint," Thomas said.

Sharp didn't deny it. Thomas looked at Spencer, then said, "You'll be the former ramrod of the D-Ring-T, right?"

Spencer nodded.

"What happened over there, Vent?" Thomas asked.

"Had to shoot Grey Taper's son, Bert," Vent said.

Thomas whistled. "No wonder the damn hills around here are full of Taper's hardcases. Hell, they been driftin' in and out of town for several days now, buying grub and likkering up at Branda's place."

Vent pointed a thumb at Sharp and said, "Owney here salted three of Taper's waddies in the Red Horse when they got a sudden seizure of the braveries and drew on him. Taper ain't too happy about it."

"And Taper killed Bowdrey," Thomas said.

"You hear about that, did ya?" Vent asked.

"I heard about it," Thomas said, and there was deep bitterness in his voice. "Shot him cold. He didn't even go for his Colt. They say Smiley Brown pulled the trigger."

"He did," Spencer said grimly.

"Some of Taper's riders have been seen talking to Branda and that gunslick of his, O'Brien," Thomas said. "I figure they struck a deal, or had one all the time. Maybe you fellers best light outta here."

"Appreciate you bringing our horses down here," Vent said, walking to the back door. "We figured to pick up some grub and head north for a while. If you see Branda around, you might just tell him that."

Thomas grinned. "I'll do her or have her done." Then he glanced at his deputy and cautioned, "You didn't hear any of this, Del. Understand?"

Nodding his understanding, the deputy moved over to the door and checked the street as Thomas said, "Go on down to the valley and tell McKiver to take his people and go home. Tell him everything's all right here and that Vent'll be along soon."

Jerking his head in an affirmative, the deputy slipped through the door and was gone. "Good man, that feller," Thomas said. "Reminds me a lot of you when you first came to work for me. Only difference is, Del ain't got near your speed, but he makes up for it in guts . . . which'll probably get the poor bastard killed before he's twenty-two," Thomas said, and there was real regret in his voice.

Vent grinned as he observed, "I've made twenty-eight. They's hope."

"You, Mr. Torrey, are a different sort of cat," Thomas said.

"Yeah, before they get old Vent in the ground, they'll have to shoot him, beat him over the head with an axe, stab him with a cavalry sword, stick him with a Bowie, and set off a few sticks of dynamite under him," Sharp observed.

"And even after that, somebody'll have to stand on his coffin lid till they get it covered with dirt," Spencer added.

Shaking his head, Thomas led them to the stable behind his office and watched them mount and ride for Jorstad's place.

"Lot of hard bark there," he said to the wall.

While Vent and his companions were riding toward Jorstad's ranch, a lone Indian riding a spotted pony moved cautiously along the base of a cliff far to the north. Every few hundred yards he stopped and sat very still while carefully looking the country over in front and to the sides of his position.

The horse was beautifully trained. When the Indian spoke to it, the animal stopped and did not move until the rider on its back clucked softly; then it slow-walked ahead, but appeared to be fully aware of its master's vigilance.

The Indian was dressed in a pair of baggy white pants made out of duck cloth and a shirt that had once been red but was now a dark brown color from an accumulation of sweat and dirt ground into the cloth by much hard usage. Around his forehead he wore a white headband that tied back long, black hair falling to his shoulders.

As he rode along, he carried a .38-40 rifle across the swells of a white man's saddle, and on his hip he wore a heavy Colt .45 issued by the army and removed from the dead body of a careless scout he had killed up in the Mogollons.

If his face wasn't so furiously set in an almost permanent scowl, he could have been considered almost handsome.

Now he dropped his right hand down to caress the butt of the .45 jutting forth from a cutaway holster suspended from a shell-heavy cartridge belt. A second belt buckled around the Indian's waist reflected gleaming rows of brass .38-40 shells.

This was the Apache Kid, one of the most feared Indians in the Southwest and a killer who had murdered half a hundred white men and several Indian women, captured by him and carried away into the mountains, then cast aside when he grew bored with them. He had a large reward on his head, a reward that was destined to remain uncollected.

Now he was in need of a grubstake and a woman. His last squaw had died after being bitten by a rattlesnake, and the Kid buried her in a shallow grave and rode away, leaving no marker and caring nothing for her loss. He knew she would be easy to replace.

As he worked his way from towering pinnacle to towering pinnacle, watching, always watching, he occasionally sniffed the wind like a dog. He could smell men, could tell the difference between an Indian's smell and a white man's.

As he rode along, every sense alert and wire tight, he thought idly of the new squaw he planned to steal. This time she would be white. He had never had a white woman, even when he worked for the white eyes' cavalry as a scout and was around a number of them at the fort. Now he would change all that. He would capture a white woman and take her to a place far up the Navajo's traditional sacred canyon north of the painted cliffs where the Chiricahua Apache made their home and sometimes came down into the valleys and killed the white ranchers and stole their cattle. He could see in his mind the sacred place with its cool stream and ancient cliff dwellings. He was not afraid of the Navajo. They were dog eaters and growers of roots, and they did not knew how to fight. Yes, it would be interesting to look upon the pure white skin of a white woman for a change, the Kid told himself and rode on with great caution, knowing he was drawing nearer and nearer to the places where white men ran their cattle.

While the Apache Kid moved southwest like a red ghost of the desert, twenty riders burst into the front yard of the Jorstad ranch and, guns blazing, killed Wag Jorstad and four of his men.

McKiver had just left the bunkhouse and gone to the barn to saddle a horse for Amelia, who had said she wished to take an evening ride and had asked McKiver to accompany her. She was currying her bay mare when the riders struck. Running to the barn door, McKiver saw Jorstad burst from the front door and lift his Colt, fire it twice, and fall as guns roared across the yard and in front of the bunkhouse. Trying to rise, the rancher was hit again and fell back, a great red stain spreading over his chest and into the dust of the yard.

A man screamed high and wild near the west end of the bunkhouse, then a shotgun roared, emptying an invader saddle. McKiver drew his gun and, turning to Amelia, said sharply, "Go. They're border jumpers—Comancheros. Out the back."

Everyone in the southwest knew of the Comancheros. They were the most feared outlaws in the desert states, riding out of nowhere, striking with sudden fury and looting a ranch, stripping it of horses and cows and women and fading back into the wild rimrock country again, defying all efforts to track them down. Only the Apache scouts who worked for Gen. George Crook had the ability to track the Comancheros.

Amelia, a child of the frontier, knew what to expect if taken prisoner by these wild desert fighters. She took one last frightened look at McKiver, who was crouched in the barn door methodically firing out into the yard, and rode north, keeping the barn and outbuildings between her and the raging gunfight at the ranch.

To the south, Vent heard the firing and drove spurs to his Appaloosa and, with Spencer and Sharp close behind him, rode for the ranch.

Ten long minutes later they galloped into the yard as McKiver and two men in the bunkhouse desperately fought for their lives. Dust boiled around the attackers' horses' hooves. The air was filled with rolling clouds of black powder and the ugly odor of cordite.

Unshucking his .44, Vent slammed a wild-looking rider from the saddle with a bullet through the chest and watched as the man tumbled into the dust screaming, his hat flying off and a tangle of black hair splayed around his head. Riding over him, Vent fired at a big man in batwing chaps, saw him flinch and sway in the saddle as his horse, reins loose, galloped into the desert, where its rider suddenly dropped free, struck the ground, and rolled several times, coming up solidly against a boulder.

Sharp fired his gun empty as three Comancheros whirled their horses to face this new menace. All three went down. One man was knocked backward over his cantleboard and the other two dropped sideways as their horses veered to avoid colliding with Sharp's mount.

Loosing a high Rebel yell, Spencer rode into and over an outlaw mounted on a small wiry desert horse. As the bay galloped past, one powerful hoof struck the rider on the skull, killing him instantly.

McKiver fired at a man sitting his horse near the corral who was leveling a rifle at Sharp's back. The man suddenly stiffened, rose on his tiptoes in the stirrups, then dropped the rifle, and, face slowly flattening out in an expressionless mask of death, pitched over his animal's neck.

Again the shotgun hammered out its challenge from the bunkhouse, and Vent saw a lean, powerful-looking man wearing a serape and a pair of crossed bandoleers literally jerked straight out and away from his saddle, where he seemed to hang in the air for a long moment before falling into the dust, a great bloody hole in the center of his chest.

Whirling his horse on its hind legs, Vent rode toward the front of the bunkhouse, where three men had dismounted and were on the verge of bursting through the door.

"Up, you bastards, up!" Vent shouted and, as they turned, shot one in the head, a second through the chest, and the third man in the stomach just as a full load of buckshot hammered through the door behind the man and caught him full in the back. One of the slugs from the heavy weapon struck the silver on Vent's saddle horn and whined away, missing him by less than three inches.

Turning his horse, he was suddenly confronted by an empty yard, except for the sprawled bodies of fourteen dead Comancheros and five Jorstad men, including Wag Jorstad.

Sharp sat his horse calmly in the middle of the carnage

and punched the empties from his Colt, then reloaded. Tucking a long slim cigar in one corner of his mouth, he lit it and inhaled deeply.

Spencer was crouching over Wag Jorstad, and now he stood and looked at Vent and shook his head.

Slowly, cautiously, McKiver came from the barn, his face black with powder, and walked to where Jorstad lay. As he knelt and had his look, a voice from the bunkhouse called out, "Hey, boss, what's goin' on out there?"

McKiver stood up and called wearily, "It's all over, boys, come on out," and waited until the door opened a crack and a double-barreled shotgun bore menaced them. "Come on ta hell out, Gimpy. It's over," he said.

A short, tough-looking rider with a gimp leg hobbled down the steps of the bunkhouse, followed by two other riders. Seeing Jorstad, he stopped and cursed.

"Yeah," McKiver agreed.

"Help, help me," a voice near the barn called.

Sharp walked over, looked down at the wounded Comanchero, a boy not more than eighteen years old, and said, "All right," and lifting his Colt, shot the boy in the left eye.

Turning, Vent had his look, turned away again, and told McKiver, "Sorry we didn't make it in time to help Wag."

"You couldn't have known," McKiver said, then suddenly whirled and looked off to the north. "Damn!" he exclaimed, "I forgot all about Amelia. I put her on a horse and told her to skedaddle. She headed north."

Going quickly to his horse, Vent stepped into the saddle and rode past McKiver. As he neared the barn, he heard one of Jorstad's men call, "Hey, Mac, this here feller usta work for Butch Hanks," but Vent did not stop. When he hit the desert, he let the big Appaloosa out into a gallop and kept him there while he followed the deep depressions left by Amelia's horse. They led away in a straight line toward the distant rimrock, and Vent thought about a lone girl out in that barren waste at night with no water and no gun.

He knew he would have to find her and find her fast.

The Apache Kid sat his horse ten feet back up the narrow cut in the cliff wall and watched the girl riding toward him. She was not the white woman he had in mind to take as his new squaw, but thinking the gods were being good to him by saving him a long ride, he decided to accept their gift.

As she passed the cut he rode out to claim it.

Amelia did not see the Apache Kid until the Indian was almost upon her, and then she knew it was too late to try and run on a played-out horse. Instead, she glanced around at him casually, nodded, and continued riding as he fell in beside her.

"Nice day," Amelia remarked, not looking at the Kid.

The Indian understood English and in fact spoke it almost as well as most white men. He had been raised on the reservation and had at one time been an army scout under Al Siebert, the famous frontiersman. Then the Kid had gone on the owlhoot trail, and when Siebert came after him, the Kid shot the scout in the leg and got away.

After that the army hired Mickey Fine, one of the frontier's greatest Apache scouts, described by Siebert once as "half Mexican, half Indian, and all son-of-a-bitch."

Fine tracked the Kid for over a year, but he too failed. Meanwhile, the Kid struck when and where he pleased and, when pursued, faded off into the Chiricahua Mountains or galloped south of the border and left his enemies with a handful of wish and a sackful of air.

Now he stared at this diminutive woman with the big eyes and the calm voice and wondered who she thought he was.

"Who you think I am?" he asked brusquely.

Glancing at him and looking straight into his eyes, she said, "I guess you're an Indian, an Apache by the looks of your clothes. My brother is . . . was Wag Jorstad . . ."

The Kid had heard of Jorstad's arrangement with his people, but he wasn't bound by any treaty or bargain struck between Apache and a white man. Grunting, he said, "I know who your brother is. My people are fools to make deals with white eyes. You people make fools of Indians. You steal our land, dig our gold, cut our timber, and rape our women. Me"—and he tapped himself on the chest—"I do the same to your people, and you are now my prisoner."

"Oh? Well, what do you plan to do? Kill me? Eat me? Rape me? What?"

He laughed. "I will do all those things. Tonight I will do to you what the white man does to our squaws, and then you will cook for me and keep my fires and mend my clothes. When I tire of you, I will kill you or sell you to the Utes or the Navajos."

She looked away, then said, "When will you sleep? If you sleep, I will kill you."

He laughed. "How can a woman kill a man if the man sleeps on top of her all night?"

Face suddenly red, she looked away and thought, I must outwit this one, but couldn't seem to come up with an idea that was even worth considering. Each time she tried to think of something the image of her brother, shot down in the ranch yard, interrupted her thoughts, and finally she gave it up and decided to wait until an opportunity presented itself.

"Do you know who I am?" he asked and in his voice she detected a certain pride.

"Why should I care? I suppose you're some big chief or other . . ."

"No chief. Something greater than any Apache chief. I am the Apache Kid," he said grandly, and he rode looking straight ahead as Amelia turned to stare at him.

She had heard the stories of the murderous Kid, as had every rancher and rider in Arizona. She knew the army had a $10,000 reward offered for him dead or alive, and she knew that not even the great Al Siebert had been able to capture him. Now she was in his hands, and recalling all the lurid tales about the Kid, she wondered vaguely if he would let her live after he finished with her. She had no illusions about her fate. He would turn her into a squaw and use her at his leisure, and when he tired of her, he would do as he had promised; sell her to another tribe as a slave or kill her, whichever he fancied the most.

"This way," he said suddenly and turned into a narrow canyon. Following him because she knew better than to run, she rode just behind his Indian pony, but tried to memorize the place where they had left the open desert.

Half a mile up the canyon, the Kid turned sharply into another cross canyon, and as they rode along, Amelia removed her scarf and let it fall. The wind whipped it away back along the canyon until it lodged in a dead bush. He looked at her, smiled, and said, "That was foolish," and slapped her in the face, knocking her off her horse. Turning, he rode back, leaned over, and jerked the scarf loose and tied it around his own neck. Then he rode back to where she sat on the ground rubbing a bruised elbow.

As he came up to her, she looked up and said, "You bastard."

Laughing, he nodded and remarked to the wind, "This one will be fun. She has guts. Al would have liked her." Then he ordered her to mount up and watched as she crawled aboard her horse.

As they started on again, she looked straight ahead and said, "I suppose you're going to torture me soon . . ." not really believing it.

He smiled. "Just as soon as we reach my camp. It's less than a mile up this canyon." He tapped his horse with his heels, and it began to trot. Amelia's horse began trotting too and she thought, traitor.

She still wasn't afraid. Her brother had taught her from the time she could barely walk that only a coward gave in to fear, and a woman had as much right to be brave as a man, maybe more so out in this tough, hard country. She did not look forward to being raped by this smelly Indian any more than another woman would have, but she also knew that if she had even a ghost of a chance of outsmarting him, she must not give way to fear. Face facts, her brother had told her. Examine what may happen. Think it out. Take it apart and analyze it. To know the source of one's fear is to be able to live and function with it, he had told her.

Deliberately examining the Kid, she saw he had powerful shoulders, that he was fairly tall for an Apache, and that his waist was narrow. He was not unhandsome. He smelled, but then, most Indians smelled in the Southwest. Water was too precious a thing to be wasted by using it on the body. Besides, the body's natural oils kept away the mosquitoes and night bugs. She knew about sex, about the mechanics of it. She had watched enough animals breed on the ranch not to understand the miracle of reproduction. She had also read books about it, which her brother had bought in Denver and quietly placed in their small library. He had not ordered her to read them, but they were there, and because he was a progressive man for that year and place, she knew what happened to a maiden on her wedding night.

Making herself think about all this, she deliberately equated the act with her and the Apache Kid, thinking, It happens to all women sooner or later, and who it happens with is important; but when one has no control over one's fate, then accepting it is the line of least resistance. She decided to make the best of it if and when he took her. She would not fight; she would not give him that pleasure.

Ahead she saw a small grove of trees, and then they were dismounting beneath them and the Kid was pulling her toward where a small spring bubbled from a crevasse in the rocks. The water was pure and cold and she lay on her stomach and drank deep, then rose and stood docilely while the Kid had his drink. While he unsaddled the horses and spread a blanket on the grass, she watched him coldly, thinking, damn him, he can't even wait until we've eaten.

As if reading her mind, he said, "When the fruit is ripe on the tree, one should pluck it before the opportunity passes." Pointing at her clothes, he ordered, "Take those off," and began to disrobe.

Watching him with hypnotic fascination, she stood, hands at her sides, feet planted wide and breath coming fast, and suddenly all her good intentions disapppeared. She could not stand here and let him do this.

Looking up, he saw she hadn't moved, and he said sharply, "Take your damn clothes off or I'll cut them off," and he picked up a wicked-looking knife and walked toward her. He was dressed only in a breechclout, and as he came at her she backed up until she was against a huge boulder and could retreat no further.

He stopped in front of her and lifted the tip of the

knife until it rested just under her chin and said in a whisper, "Take them off or die now."

Sobbing softly and hating herself for it, she slowly removed her shirt and skirt and then let fall her underclothes. As he stepped back, he reached down and tossed off his breechclout and stood naked before her.

She looked down at herself clothed now only in her underpants and chemise, and could not bring herself to remove them. Walking to her, he laughed and said, "All white women are shy. Come," and pulling her along, he pushed her down on the blanket, straddled her, and ripped away her remaining clothing. As her naked body came into view, he stared at it for a long time, then using his knee, forced her thighs apart and dropped between them. Staring up at him and almost nauseated by his smell, she turned her head and closed her eyes, ordering herself, willing herself to relax, to accept what she couldn't help. Then he began forcing himself into her and she screamed and one arm whipped back and the hand found a fist-sized boulder, picked it up, and swung it around with strength born of desperation, connecting solidly with the Kid's forehead.

As the satisfying crack signified she had struck accurately, he suddenly went limp and with a long, gusty sigh rolled away from her and onto his back. Rising shakily, she looked down at him then found her clothing and dressed hurriedly. Removing a rope from his saddle, she quickly hog-tied the unconscious Indian. Then she calmly saddled her horse and, picking up his rifle, shoved it into the scabbard. Draping his shell belts and pistol belt from her saddle horn, she gathered up his clothing and tied it behind his cantleboard, then saddled his horse. The Indian pony, not liking her smell, jerked away until she rapped it smartly on the nose with a stick and said harshly, "Stand still, you slab-sided bastard," wondering where she had heard that.

Ready to leave, she walked over, filled her canteen, and then stood over the Kid and very carefully examined his naked body. It was the first time she had ever seen a naked man up this close, and she thought rather inanely, They're kinda pretty.

Then she rode from the canyon, leading the Kid's horse, and began backtracking toward the desert.

Five miles from the entrance to the canyon where the Kid lay ignobly trussed like a pig waiting for the spit, and by a woman at that, Vent Torrey urged his tired horse on.

Eyes traversing the side canyons and occasionally dropping to recheck Amelia's horse's tracks, he hoped she hadn't gone too far.

That fight at the Jorstad place had been a wild one, he told himself and then recalled how Sharp had cold-bloodedly shot the young wounded Comanchero in the head. Vent wondered how far down the trail he must travel before he became that calloused. He knew Sharp was not a hateful man. He had killed the boy because that was how he played the game. Vent knew Sharp was right, that the man who gave an enemy a break would someday wake up along the trail and find that enemy drinking his coffee and staring at him over the barrel of a six-shooter just before he pulled the trigger. Still, he had never killed that way. He did not think he could. It was no use telling himself that they would have hanged the boy anyway if he lived and that Sharp did him a favor. Sharp had not killed as a favor. He killed because of his own creed, a creed that Vent knew he must someday adopt or die. As his reputation grew, more and more of the young foolish ones would come for their try at adding his reputation to their mediocre ones. If he let one of them walk away, that one might be the man who would gain by his first foolish mistake and return again, this time with the expertise to finish the job.

Raising his head, he gazed into nothingness and wondered why he should be saddled with such a future. All his life he had used guns and known death and hate, but other men had lived in the same climate and had moved out from under it and gone away and become something else and were forgotten. Vent had not. Instead, he was his father's son. Thinking back on that hard Missourian, he could easily understand why he was the way he was. The feud had done most of it. His family and the Hawks family had killed each other for over a hundred years. They became so proficient at killing that no one crossed them, no one wanted their society. They lived among themselves, not because that was the kind of life they preferred, but because other men shunned them.

William Torrey was the last family head when he moved his wife, daughter, and three sons to Kansas. The Hawks had followed, and old man Hawks, the last remaining head of that family, had lain in wait with his oldest son on the road to Dodge City and had shot Vent's father through the body. William Torrey had ridden several miles to the ranch with half an inch shot away from the lower part of his heart and managed to live four days before he died.

Thinking back on what happened next set Vent's hand to itching. The Hawks had come to the ranch one early spring morning, and in the savage gunfight that followed, both his brothers had taken fatal wounds and he wound up being hauled away west in a wagon with a hole in his body and a smashed gunhand.

In Colorado he saved the life of an Indian boy, and the boy's father, a sachem of the Ute tribe, presented Vent with the Appaloosa he still rode and the leather contraption for his shattered hand that was indirectly the cause of his turning to guns as a way of life. The leather straps he wore on his hand had somehow improved it beyond its prior capabilities, and constant practice had developed a natural speed and eye that could match the best.

Before it was over, Vent had killed all the Hawks except old Hitch, and he left him with a mangled gunhand in an ironic twist of fate. Vent could have killed the old man then, but instead he rode out.

Now as he followed Amelia's tracks into a canyon, he wondered if he had made a mistake he someday would regret. Maybe he should have killed the last of the Hawks and been done with it.

Because of the feud and his winning it, his name had become a household word in the West, pushing him into gun jobs that led to more killings.

Vent Torrey had killed more than twenty men, and he was only twenty-eight years old.

Looking up at a sudden sound, he saw Amelia riding toward him leading an Indian pony and calmly gazing around her if trying to remember where the trail was. Vent pulled in and waited until she came up and stopped, then said, "Miss Amelia, you all right?"

"I'm fine, Mr. Torrey." Nodding toward the Indian pony, she said, "Back up this here canyon a ways they's a 'Pache all nice and tied up and waiting to be hauled away. He said he was the Apache Kid."

"Tied up?"

"Yep, tied up. He tried to . . . well," she broke off and her face turned red as she looked at him and suddenly remembered how she had left the Indian and wondered what this tall calm-faced man with the piercing brown eyes would think of her once he saw the Kid.

Rolling a cigarette as he thought over her words, he finally nodded as if he understood and said, "Let's go have a look see. If he's the Kid, you're ten thousand dollars richer."

Then she remembered the fight at the ranch and looked at him from eyes that threatened to spill over and asked, "Wag?"

"I'm sorry, ma'am," he said and meant it.

Without a word, she led the way back to the spring and just short of the woods drew in and, pointing, said, "Back in there they's a little spring. I left him there," and watched as Vent cautiously rode into the trees, trying to look everywhere at once. He knew that just because Amelia had left the Kid tied didn't necessarily mean he was still in that condition.

He was right. When he reached the spring, the Indian was gone. Vent had his careful look at the sign, read it clearly, and then turned and walked his horse back to where the girl waited and said, "He's lit out. It figures. That feller's as slippery as a bar of cowboy soap."

"But I left him tied up," Amelia protested.

"He got loose," Vent said. "Probably should have plugged him."

She stared at him wide-eyed. "But he was unconscious," she protested.

"Don't matter. He's the Apache Kid. They ain't no rules when it comes to that feller," Vent said and led the way back down the canyon.

"Damn," she exclaimed, and Vent grinned to himself, thinking, my but she's fiesty.

While Vent rode toward the Jorstad ranch with Amelia, far to the east near the town of Dry Springs a big, powerful white-haired man strode up and down his veranda while several of his riders waited in his yard.

"I don't see this feller Leatherhand tied to anybody's saddle," Grey Taper said. "In fact, nobody's seen him except a couple of you tavern bums, and I'm not sure I even believe that. I think you're chasing a ghost. I think it was a ghost who killed Bert. It wasn't a man at all. It had to be a ghost. Only a ghost could hide from fifty men . . ."

Cole Butram rose from where he had been squatting near the steps and said quietly, "The boys saw him in the Devil's Rondeevoo in Jerome. I believe them."

"Then why ain't he here now?" Taper insisted.

"He got away. That's the way of it," Butram said.

Taper stared at them, then said sharply, "Get my horse. I'm riding out with you. Guess a feller has to stomp his own snakes."

"What about Sharp and Spencer?" Smiley Brown asked.

"We catch them, we hang them," Taper snapped.

Chapter V

A light wind touched the girl's hair and lifted it off her neck for just a moment, then capriciously shifted directions and tilted her hat brim upward, making her look like a very young cavalry trooper with too-long hair.

Vent watched her and wondered what had happened up in that gulch with the Apache Kid. Whatever it was, he figured it would make a hell of a story to tell his grandchildren, if he lived long enough to have any, which he doubted.

"The Kid must have been some mad to find himself outfoxed by a woman," Vent chuckled.

"He didn't have a chance," Amelia said with a quiet smile. "I just sorta knocked him into the middle of next week with a rock while he was otherwise occupied, then tied him up before he woke. When I left, he was resting easy just a-waiting for someone to come gather him up."

"Pretty slippery feller," Vent commented, watching the edges of pinnacles and cuts in the desert where men might lurk in ambush.

Turning her head she stared at him, then asked, "You believe me, don't you?"

"Yes, ma'am. Sign backed you up, and then there's all

that gear. You wouldn't have it unless your story was true."

She seemed relieved and was about to make another comment when a dozen riders suddenly rode up out of a low wash three hundred yards away and headed toward them. Taper's men, Vent thought and, turning the Appaloosa sharply, said, "Taper's boys. You go on. They won't do you a hurt. It's me they want." And when she would have argued, he snapped, "No. Unless you wanta watch a hanging, you ride on."

Looking at him helplessly, she started to say something else, but he whirled the big horse and put the spurs to him. Glancing back, he watched the line of riders push their horses to a gallop.

He wondered how fresh their animals were. He knew how fresh the Appaloosa was. Another look back showed him two riders reining up to slide to a stop on each side of Amelia. One bent and took the reins from her while the other rode alongside and relieved her of the Kid's weapons. Vent wasn't worried. No cowboy in his right mind would harm a woman in that part of the country. Any man who did was immediately outlawed and every other man's target. And when caught usually never made it to jail. Instead such men were invited to a necktie party as the guest of honor and left dangling at the end of a rope.

The riders behind Vent had not gained on him but were not falling behind either. The pace was steady and Vent knew he could keep away from them. What he didn't think he could do was outrun them, not on the Appaloosa. The big horse was done in. He had been ridden all day and now was being asked to give yet a little more. When Vent wheeled east along the base of the towering cliffs, he saw the big Appaloosa begin to slug its head and knew he either had to quit or kill the horse.

Behind him an over-eager rider fired a rifle. The bullet droned past Vent's ear. He ignored it. For a man to hit another with a rifle at that distance, and both of them riding full out, would be a miracle. Vent figured if his luck was that bad, he was probably done for anyway.

Then the Appy stumbled, caught itself, and floundered on, but Vent could feel the muscles giving out as the big horse gave his best.

"To hell with it," he said and watched the mouth of a narrow canyon loom up ahead. When he came even with it, he wheeled the horse sharply into it and dragged a last burst of speed from him, making the upper end. Half a mile from the entrance he heard a shout and then pulled the Appaloosa in. Jerking his rifle and canteen free, he dropped to the ground and ran into a cross canyon, leaving the dead-beat horse standing in the middle of the wash, his head down and eyes bright with exhaustion.

Fifty feet along the cross canyon, he found a tunnel-like aperture leading north and dodged into it. He was just in time. Taper's riders burst into the canyon behind him, and as he dashed along the narrow cut, he heard them shouting to one another, apparently having missed his escape route. He knew they would find it again, but it bought him some time.

The further along the crack he ran the narrower it became, and he offered up a silent prayer that it wouldn't just end slam up against a cliff face, knowing if that happened he might hold them off and even cut their number in half, but sooner or later they'd winkle him out and either capture or kill him. The crack kept going.

Another ten minutes and he heard their first discovery shout behind him and thought grimly that it wouldn't be long until they reached the narrow beginning of his bolt hole and left their horses.

For five minutes he had been running on solid rock, then suddenly he was facing several spur cracks leading in half a dozen directions. All of them were of a size and all had stone floors. Flipping a mental coin, he decided to stay with the one he was in and kept going straight ahead. Fifty feet more and it spread out again like the fingers on a hand. This time he chose a secondary crack that turned into a tunnel a hundred feet further on. Ducking, he continued, hoping against hope it didn't run out on him.

As he made his way along the narrow tunnel, he figured it must be over 100 degrees in that place and knew that if he didn't take on some water soon, he would pass out from the heat. Stopping, he uncorked the canteen, lifted it to his mouth and took a short pull, then reluctantly replaced the cap, having no idea how long it must last him. He only knew of three waterholes in all that desert, and they were beyond his reach and probably guarded by Taper's men.

Far behind him he heard a shout then several answering shouts and wondered if his pursuers had split up. He doubted it. No one of them would take a chance on meeting him face to face in one of those narrow cracks in the rock.

At that point, the tunnel began to close in and another fifty feet found him bent over, moving ahead very slowly. It seemed like hours before the tunnel again began to widen and then became large enough for him to stand. His back and legs ached with the strain, but he thought, what the hell, it's better than swinging from a damn rope or going down with a gut full of Taper lead.

Then he saw light ahead and very cautiously moved to where the tunnel opened into a wide, green meadow completely enclosed by rock cliffs. At the far end a small spring bubbled from a hole, its cool water spreading over the meadow and nurturing the grass. A deer suddenly lifted its head and stared over a shoulder at Vent, then walked off along the face of the cliff and into a small stand of trees.

Stepping boldly into the opening Vent said, "Well, I'll be damned, what the hell is this?"

After refilling his canteen and refreshing himself at the spring, he made a circle around the meadow and discovered it was rock-locked, with the only entrance the one he had come through. Near the spring he did find a set of crude steps leading up the face of the cliff, and standing looking toward the late afternoon sky, he hoped he wouldn't have to make a try at leaving the meadow by that route.

His stomach told him he had missed too many meals, and he gazed at the deer longingly, but knew that to fire his gun would be to send an invitation to Taper's men. Even if they couldn't place the shot in these tangled canyons, they would know he was further west and by walking out each tunnel would eventually find him. He rolled a smoke instead.

As he lay by the spring smoking, he wondered what his next move should be. Trying to put himself in the pursuer's place he figured they would make camp in the canyon where he had left the Appaloosa and send somebody for more water and supplies and then wait him out. Sooner or later he must quit or die. Meanwhile, they could go on carefully investigating each of the finger canyons.

Stoically gazing at the sky, Vent accepted his plight, knowing that sometimes waiting was the best remedy. He waited.

Then the rabbit hopped out from behind a small

growth of mesquite and he stared at it in wonder as it went about its business as if he weren't there. Slowly he sat up, picked up a rock from the gravel around the spring, and, taking careful aim, flung it at the animal with all his strength. The long-eared creature's sixth sense smelled the danger a split second before the rock reached it. It leaped clear, then whirled and in its fright ran straight toward Vent. As it passed, he reached out a long arm, grabbed it by the ears, and, with a quick whipping motion, broke its neck.

Half an hour later the rabbit was roasting over a small, smokeless fire. Its smell permeated the box canyon, and Vent forced himself to wait until it was finished cooking.

When it was done he ate it all, peeling the meat away from the white bones and then cracking the bones and licking out the marrow. He chased it down with icy spring water, and when there was no more he sat back, rolled a smoke, and grinned. For the first time since Taper's men popped up out of the desert he figured he might live to see another day.

Cleaning up the evidence of his meal, he walked to the grove of trees and, crawling in among the low bushes surrounding their butts, went immediately to sleep. When he awoke it was dark and his mouth felt as if a troop of Piutes had camped in it. A pale three-quarter moon threw its light into the meadow, and when Vent crawled forth, the deer, feeding very close to the trees, suddenly snorted and broke away along the floor of the box canyon; then Vent heard its hooves strike rock and cursed as he guessed it had gone into the tunnel. He knew if it kept going, it would eventually run right into Taper's men, who would quickly guess there was water back along that tunnel.

Walking down to the entrance he stood back and examined it in the moonlight and decided he could probably hold it for a long time against even a determined bunch of men, but that sooner or later somebody would decide to get above him and then it would be like shooting fish in a well bucket. That's when he decided to wait until first light then attempt the steps. The deer had left him no choice.

He made his wait leaning against the rock wall near the spring, and when the day's first glimmer of light came, following the moon's sudden disappearance, leaving the canyon a black hole of nothingness, he went and had a final long drink, then put his boot toe to the bottom step and started up. It was slow, painful, and dangerous. Once, when his boot lost its precarious purchase, he almost fell into the canyon. Holding on so tight he became dizzy, he waited a good five minutes in order to regain the strength to go on.

It required almost an hour of back-breaking labor to reach the top, but finally Vent slid onto flat ground on his stomach and lay panting and shivering. He had been forced to leave his rifle in the canyon, hidden in the trees, because he couldn't figure a way to strap it on his back. Thinking about it now, he was glad he hadn't tried it. He would have had to abandon it long before he reached the top. Once, after he almost fell, he seriously considered unbuckling his handgun and letting it fall, but changed his mind when he thought about having to bend over and undo the tiedown. At that moment someone called and Vent rolled away from the edge of the cliff and lay still. He could hear the sound of men scrambling through the rocky tunnel and then someone shouted, "Hey, Smiley. Look what I found. A spring."

Several men gathered below where Vent lay, and as he eavesdropped, he could hear their canteens banging against the rocks.

"Where the hell you reckon that hombre got to?" Smiley asked.

"Well, he sure as hell didn't fly outta here," a man said.

"If he didn't come in here, then what the hell spooked that deer so bad?" someone else wanted to know.

"Anybody check out that bunch of trees over there?" Smiley asked and there was sudden tension in his voice, followed by the loud sound of several single action pistols being placed on full cock.

Nobody said anything, then a man called from the grove. "Hey, Smiley, they's a rifle in here."

"Well, bring the damn thing out," Smiley ordered irritably.

More silence.

Sounds of pistols being uncocked.

A canteen rattled on the rock.

"That rifle ain't been here very long," Smiley said, and then somebody worked the lever action on it and Vent heard the tinny sound of an ejected shell striking the rocks.

"Where the hell did he go if he ain't in this canyon?" somebody asked.

"Hey, here's a set of steps going up the cliff," a man called from near the spring.

Smiley cursed and snarled, "Get the hell back against the face of the rock," and the command was followed by scrambling sounds, the clatter of a pistol barrel against rock, and then silence settled on the box canyon.

Vent knew he could hold the top of the cliff forever, but without food and only one canteen, he'd have to run sooner or later. He did not know how many of Taper's men were in the box canyon but guessed by the sound of their voices Smiley had split his forces, leaving half of them down at the tunnel entrance and bringing the rest into the box canyon.

Crawling away from the lip of the cliff, Vent slowly stood up and carefully walked away, moving north along the tablelike top of the upthrust wedge of red rock. Two hours later he was still going and none of Taper's men had come after him. All gurgle and no guts, he thought and tramped on grimly, nursing his water and watching for a way down off the tabletop.

All that day he moved north. Once he thought he had come to the end of his string when the rimrock began to narrow alarmingly. When it reached a place where it was less than five feet wide and beginning to take on the shape of a camel's back, it abruptly ended. Walking to the edge he stared across at the next plateau and tried to estimate the distance between the two. Five feet, he told himself and knew he was going to have to try it or retrace his steps straight into Smiley's hands.

Moving back until there were thirty feet between him and the edge, he allowed himself a small drink, then carefully capped the canteen and double slung it over his shoulder. He did not want to lose it down some cliff.

Ducking his head he ran straight along the cliff top and leaped. His boots struck solidly, then he stumbled forward and pitched onto his side, skinning his elbow and shoulder on the rough stone. Sitting up, he grimaced painfully but offered up a prayer to whatever god was watching over him and regained his feet. Walking back to the edge he looked down the sheer face of a drop that had to be at least three hundred feet.

Night found him moving east. The plateau had suddenly become a huge L, and where it went he had to follow. Because the moon provided good traveling light, he kept going, grateful for the cooler air, until almost midnight when it started to get really cold. The desert was like that, he knew—freezing a man at night and boiling him during the day.

When he could go no farther, he lay down and slept on the hard rock, waking the following morning all aches and pains, his peeled elbow and skinned shoulder infected and giving him the willies. He had another drink, and then, holding the canteen up, he shook it and cursed at the barely audible sound of less than a cup of water sloshing around in the bottom. He wondered how long a man could live in that wasteland without water. He had heard of men who went for several days and of others who died the third and sometimes even the second day. He guessed he was going to get his chance to find out.

His water ran out at about the same time he discovered a way off the plateau. A huge slide of jumbled boulders piled one on top of the other afforded him a precarious path to the desert floor, probably dumped there when some mighty cataclysm struck this land and tore it asunder thousands of years before the advent of man. Slowly, gingerly, he moved down the rock slide, crawling from boulder to boulder, checking each for stability and watching where he placed his boots. He did not want to wind up with a foot caught in a crevasse and no way to extricate it.

He was halfway down when he heard the snake give its warning rattle. Standing very still, he slowly turned his head, looking for the deadly creature. When he saw it he relaxed. It lay on a rock ten feet from him, too far away to do him any harm. He grinned and said through cracked lips, "Old snake, I ain't about to move onto your territory," and continued on down.

When he finally gained the desert floor, he moved in under an overhang of the cliff and slowly lowered himself until his back was against the rock. Even in the shade he guessed the temperature must be close to 110 degrees.

When he caught himself dozing, he struggled to his feet and moved east, following a rough wagon track that he stumbled on a hundred yards out from the cliff base. It hadn't been used in years according to the way he read the sign, but he figured it had to go somewhere so he stayed with it, sometimes staggering and almost falling when the sand became an obstacle where the wind had blown it across the crude road. He didn't know how long he walked that day, but somewhere between the cliff base and the disappearance of the sun in the west he became aware of his surroundings and realized he had been walking for miles without conscious effort. Stopping then, he gazed blearily around, his eyes focusing and other times refusing to cooperate with him. He felt dry clear down to his toes and figured by the way his clothes hung on him he must have lost a good fifteen pounds.

Looking down at the heavy gunbelt, he let his hand drop to the buckle but then removed it stubbornly. Without the gun he would surely be dead if he ran up against Taper's men. Then he laughed a hollow laugh, realizing that even if he had the gun he would play hell sighting it on anything. Still, it was a part of him he refused to abandon, and even though it grew heavier and heavier the further he walked, it stayed at his hip, its smooth butt a resting place for his leather-covered right hand.

When darkness fell and turned the desert into a bleak, moon-swept landscape of odd shadows and towering rocks off which the pale light reflected in eerie lancelike slivers, Vent stopped and laid down, immediately falling asleep.

He awoke cold and shivering and rose and trudged on,

his eyes seeing only the narrow wagon ruts that seemed to lead forever across the vast expanse of sand, rock, and stunted brush. Once he saw a barrel cactus near a big rock and thought it was a man. Drawing his pistol he leveled it and said hoarsely, "Come out of there, old son, and let's have a look," and then realized he was talking to nothing and shoved the gun back in leather and trudged on.

It was morning. Vent lay huddled against a rock, shivering. When the sun came up it found him there and slowly warmed his body until its direct rays reached his eyes and woke him. Sitting back against the boulder he gazed around blearily and wondered how the hell he had managed to survive this long. Then his eye fell on one of the barrel cactus and he suddenly remembered something that had been nagging at him since he had mistaken one for a man the night before. An old prospector who had roamed all over the Arizona deserts once told him the barrel cactus contained moisture and that if you cut it open and sucked the pulp it could save your life. He had also warned that it tasted like hell and didn't last very long.

Staggering to his feet, Vent fumbled out his knife, dropped it, and almost fell over when he leaned down to retrieve it. Then he couldn't seem to locate it in the sand. Cursing in a slow monotone, he kept hunting until he finally felt the hot warmth of metal and with the knife firm in his grasp made his way to the barrel cactus. Opening the blade with great difficulty, he cut the top off the plant. Then he shoved his hand deep into the pulpy interior and brought up a handful and began sucking thirstily at it. As he felt the precious fluid touch his tongue he almost started crying with the emotion of it. Over the years he had heard men talk of going without water for several days and the horror, but until now he had never realized just how terrible the lack of enough moisture to sustain life really was. It wasn't the dying that was so bad. Hell, every man died. It was the driving, all-consuming need that was the hardest to accept. That anything in the world could render a man so impotent had always been beyond Vent's comprehension, but now he realized he would have sold his very soul for a drink if the devil himself had appeared and offered to make a deal.

It required over an hour of digging out pulp and sucking it dry before his thirst was sufficiently allayed for him to again seek shade and rest.

Half an hour later he was walking again. It was easier now. The little moisture he had managed to suck from the cactus seemed to have cleared up his vision and put new strength in his legs. Four hours later he was in as bad a condition as before he had found the cactus. His throat ached with its driving demand for water, and his legs seemed to buckle and threaten to fail him with every other step. His back felt as if someone had placed a hot branding iron on it and went away and left it there to sizzle. The sun beat down through the crown of his Stetson, slowly boiling his brains, and after a while he thought they would surely begin bubbling out his ears.

He started crawling just before dark. He crawled until almost midnight, then he stopped and it was while lying there in the trail that he heard the soft mutter of hooves coming from the direction of Dry Springs. Wildly thrashing to his feet, driven by the fear that these were Taper's riders coming, he staggered off the trail and tripped and fell heavily near some bushes. The riders came on and then pulled rein opposite where he lay and one of them said, "I could have swore something ran across the trail right here."

"Maybe a damned 'Pache," another voice growled,

and Vent heard the *snick* of a gun whipped from leather and the loud metallic click as it was eared to full cock.

One of the men dismounted, knelt, and had his look at the trail, then rose and turning, said carefully, "A man just passed here, Harp, not more'n two minutes ago."

"'Pache?" the other asked and Vent heard the first man slide his rifle free from its scabbard and cock it.

"Nope, feller wearing boots. Sand's still seeping back in the tracks. Hell, he can't be far, and if he's afoot he needs help."

"What if he's laying out there with a gun on us?" the man called Harp asked.

"Then the son-of-a-bitch will just have to shoot," the other man said and started walking toward Vent, who had slowly sat up, drawn his gun, and was now leaning against a small boulder with the heavy weapon braced on his bent knee, pointing toward the approaching men.

When the first man came within ten feet of Vent, he said hoarsely, "Reckon that's far enough, neighbor."

The man stopped short. The second man almost bumped into him. "What the hell we got here, Carl?" he asked sharply.

"Put a name to yourselves," Vent said and now he wished to hell they would hurry it because the pistol was beginning to feel as if it were an artillery field piece.

"Mister, they ain't no need for that gun. I'm Harp Sinclair and I own the Red Horse Saloon in Dry Springs. This here's Carl Shipley. He runs the Jinglebob Cafe."

Vent sighed and let the gun fall to his side and said wearily, "One of you boys happen to have a canteen with you?"

"Get a canteen," Sinclair ordered sharply, then bent and had his look at Vent and whistled. "You're Vent Torrey, ain't ya . . . or what's left of ya?"

"Ain't enough to provide even a good hanging," Vent

said and greedily gulped down half a dozen swallows of water when Shipley held the canteen to his mouth.

"How far you come without water?" he asked.

"How far we from Dry Springs?" Vent countered.

"About six miles," Sinclair said.

Accepting more water, he swallowed and slowly began to relax as the cool wetness ran into his empty stomach and was sucked up by his stomach lining and sent racing out into all the byways of his body. He thought he could actually feel it spreading as he said, "I went afoot somewhere east of the Verde Valley . . . about twenty miles from Jerome . . . ran dry the end of the second day . . . tried barrel cactus . . ."

The two men stared at each other in the moonlight, then Sinclair whistled in amazement. "Feller, you come almost two hundred miles across that desert, and it better than a hundred degrees. Christ!"

Shipley said quietly, "You know, Mr. Torrey, Taper's still after you. He's offered a five-thousand-dollar reward . . ."

"You fellers aiming on collecting?" Vent asked and somehow didn't give a damn now.

"Earl Bowdrey was my friend," Shipley said. "I was there when Taper ordered him murdered like some damn cow in a slaughtering pen. I won't forget that."

"We're gonna have to be real careful on this, Carl," Sinclair warned. "If Taper finds out we helped him, he'll send us along after Bowdrey to help shovel coal."

They helped Vent to his feet, and when he couldn't seem to find his holster to put away the gun, Sinclair did it for him, carefully hooking the thong tiedown over the hammer so he wouldn't lose it during the ride. With Vent hanging on behind him, Shipley led the way back toward Dry Springs. Two miles from town he turned into a deep wash and followed it for three miles to a small cabin tucked away between two huge rocks that hid it from casual observation. Near the building a small corral held three saddle horses, and Vent, half-asleep on Shipley's shoulder, thought about the Appaloosa and wondered if Smiley Brown ended up with him. All the more reason to kill him, he thought, and then they were dismounting at the cabin. As they half walked, half carried Vent up the porch steps and onto the veranda a woman's voice snapped a challenge from inside the house. "Who's out there. Sing away or I'll turn this scattergun loose through the damn door."

"Easy, May," Sinclair called. "It's just me and Carl. We got a man here needs attention."

"All men need attention," the voice observed waspishly, and chuckling at this sally, they carried Vent inside. Following the woman's instructions, they put the tall gunman on a bed near the south wall.

The woman walked over and said, "Where the hell did you fish this one up from?"

"That there is Leatherhand," Sinclair said almost proudly, as if he had cast a fishing line into the desert sands and caught the biggest fish of all.

"'Pears some used," she said, leaning over Vent and looking at his face beneath the lamplight. "Where'd ya dredge him up from?"

"You probably won't believe this, but that crazy feller walked, crawled, and staggered all the way from Verde Valley to about six miles from here, and he did most of it on an empty canteen and no grub, which reminds me, you got any soup stock around?"

Sighing, the woman walked to the stove and removed the lid of a large pot. "I always got soup around. Seems like that's all my customers ever want once they get what they came for. Soup!"

"You know Taper wants this hombre pretty badly?" Sinclair asked.

"I know. I wouldn't give Taper the sweat off my . . . well . . . I owe that bastard and I owe this feller for killing that no good Bert, him that use'ta come out here and beat the hell outta me and take what he wanted for nothin'. Damn animal."

"Can we leave him here with you, May?" Shipley asked.

Looking at them for a minute, her eyes suddenly softened as she said, "Sure. Hell, this is you fellers' house and you ain't never charged me a buffalo for it. You ain't tried to take her out in trade either. I don't forget them that does right by May. Hell yes, he's safe here." She ladled up a bowlful of soup and went to the bed only to discover that the object of all the talk was sound asleep.

Looking down at him the woman drew in a breath and said, "I ain't had anything that pretty in my bed for a coon's age."

Grey Taper sat in the Devil's Rondeevoo and sullenly gulped straight whiskey. Half a dozen D-Ring-T riders occupied tables around the room or lounged at the bar. Taper sat alone.

Near the front door Marshal Boots Thomas quietly drank a glass of beer that was more foam than body and mused on what the big white-haired rancher would do next. His men had apparently told him they had trapped and lost Vent Torrey somewhere out in the wasteland east of Verde Valley.

Now Taper raised his head and glared at Smiley Brown. "You say this Leatherhand was afoot, that he didn't have no horse?"

"That's right, Mr. Taper," Brown answered. He did not

like the way the big rancher was looking at him. "I got that Appaloosa of his right here in the stable."

Thomas rose and strolled down the long room and stopped at Taper's table. When the big man looked up, the marshal allowed his coat to fall back so that the rancher could see his badge, then said quietly, "I just happen to overhear your man there," and he jerked a thumb at Brown. "He admitted he stole another man's horse. Now, I don't know what you fellers over to Dry Springs do when you catch a horse thief, but over here we usually have a nice legal trial and then a hanging."

Taper stared at him. "Who the hell are you?" he snapped.

Thomas grinned. The grin did not quite reach his eyes. Taper, who had had several drinks, now suddenly decided he had better take a harder rein on his sobriety before this cold-eyed man did something foolish, like throwing down on him.

"I'm Marshal Boots Thomas, late of Cripple Creek, Colorado, and points north," Thomas said.

Smiley strutted forward and, tossing the marshal a scornful look, asked, "You want me to comb out this old rooster's feathers for ya, boss?"

Thomas cocked his head to one side while utter stillness took possession of the saloon as every Jerome man in there drew in a slow, controlled breath and prepared to hit the floor when the shooting erupted.

"Mr. Brown, I can spot you three seconds and still punch six slugs right dead center into your guts," Thomas said mildly.

Taper, small bells of alarm going off in the back of his mind, held up his hand and said brusquely, "None of that, Smiley. This here's the marshal of Jerome and as such deserves respect. We ain't outlaws. We regard the law with all due honor."

"Bull!" Thomas said conversationally. "Earl Bowdrey was a friend of mine, Mr. Taper. In fact, he had friends all over Arizona. When you had this peckerwood"—and Thomas again aimed a stubby thumb at Brown—"shoot him in cold blood, you bought more enemies in a few seconds than you could make in half a lifetime really trying."

"He had his chance," Taper said. "He received his invite. He chose not to come to the street."

Looking around at the assembled men, Thomas allowed his eyes to rest on Branda for a long moment, then moved on to push a spare glance at Von O'Brien, who stared back with just the hint of a smile playing around his full lips.

Not taking his eyes off O'Brien, Thomas observed, "Mr. Branda, you operate in this town at my sufferance. If Mr. Taper or his riders are here an hour from now I'll close you down. Understood?"

Branda moved out from the bar as O'Brien dropped a hand to his bone-handled six-shooter. He wore only one today, and it was slanted far forward in an awkward position, its butt a difficult thing to grasp. Thomas wondered at that.

"Mr. O'Brien, the moment your hand snags that pistolo, I'm going to kill you," Thomas said, then casually added, "you, up on the balcony, lay that shotgun down on the floor and leave . . . Now!"

Every eye in the saloon suddenly moved upward to stare at the guard who was carefully depositing his weapon on the floor and backing out through the door behind the balcony.

Face red, Branda said sharply, "This here's some sandy you're runnin', Mr. Marshal. Standing here all alone trying to throw a bluff into a whole saloon full of gents . . . you can't bulldoze me."

Thomas smiled. His eyes remained a cold, opaque blue. "You underestimate the boys in this here town, Mr. Branda. They sorta believe in fair and honest play. You turn your wolves loose and you'll all hang, including that big hoorah from over Dry Springs way."

Taper slowly stood, and as his men fell in behind him facing Thomas, he said, "We've leaving, Mr. Thomas."

"Fine, just so you leave Mr. Torrey's horse at the stables," Thomas said. "I understand he has a sister over around Crested Butte way whose married to a former sheriff. Feller once told me that man could beat Wyatt Earp to the gun and had one of the nastiest tempers in Colorado. If old Leatherhand's really hung up his saddle, I was you, I'd sorta grow me a pair of eyes in the back of my head."

Taper pointed a long finger at Thomas and snapped, "That pistol fighter corralled my boy into going for a gun then plugged him. I aim to balance the scales, Mr. Thomas. Whether you or his gunswift brother-in-law like it or not, if the desert didn't get him, I will, and I'll hang him high."

"You're son asked for what he got, Mr. Thomas, and you know it. He sure as hell was nothing to trade for a man like Earl Bowdrey . . ."

A frown passed over Taper's face, then he wheeled and led his men through the front door. Thomas continued to watch O'Brien, who was standing seemingly completely relaxed. The marshal wasn't fooled. As the two men stared at each other several local businessmen suddenly came together at the end of the room, and one of them, a foreman at the Little Daisy Mine, said sharply, "You listen up, Branda. You start anything with the marshal and I'll make this place off-limits to every man jack at the Daisy, and I'll get the other mine owners and businessmen of this city to follow along. You want to stay in the saloon game you play it straight."

Thomas held up his hand, and when the townsmen turned to look at him, he said quietly, "Thanks, boys. I think Mr. Branda gets the idea."

O'Brien suddenly folded his hands across his chest and stared blandly at Thomas as the marshal nodded swiftly and turned his back and walked out the front door. He was in time to watch the Taper men ride out. As Grey Taper moved his horse past the marshal, he turned his head and looked down at him, and Thomas looked back and said nothing.

Five miles along the stage road to the Jorstad ranch, Taper reined in and, stepping off his big bay, walked over to Smiley Brown, reached long powerful arms up, and suddenly jerked him bodily from the saddle and hurled him into the dirt. Scrambling wildly, Brown scuttled to the edge of the track but was not fast enough to avoid a savage boot Taper planted in his short ribs. Grunting in agony, Brown managed to reach his feet, ran back a short distance and whirled, going for his gun with a vicious oath.

He never cleared leather. Cole Butram drew like lightning and shot him through the body, the big .45 slug jerking him off his feet and hurling him backward. Brown hit the ground with an agonized grunt, his face twisted in horror, then screamed once and died.

"He always was a two-bitter," Butram observed, punching out the empty shell and replacing it from his gunbelt.

Taper walked over and looked down at the dead man, shook his head, and turning away, said, "One of you boys get his horse. We've got a long ride," and mounted and led the men off into the desert.

A fly settled on Brown's face, buzzed contentedly, and

then flew away, allowing the slightest breeze to carry him toward a stand of ancient trees fifty feet off the road.

Butch Hanks was not interested in flies. He was interested in acquiring the Jorstad ranch and figured he was damn close to accomplishing it. There was one obstacle left now that Leatherhand was apparently finished. That obstacle was McKiver. Hanks told himself McKiver had to die. The question was, how to accomplish it without the least amount of fuss? What with all the killing going on in that part of Arizona, Hanks knew sooner or later the army would show up and martial law would be declared. He also knew army types were notoriously short-tempered when it came to small and big infractions of their rules. They held drum-head courts and strung people to telegraph poles, or threw them into jails, and then presided over local courts that usually sentenced the defendants to long periods of incarceration at Yuma, the hellhole of all hellhole prisons in the southwest.

Hanks did not want to go to Yuma. He did not want the army to come anywhere near Jerome. Thinking about it now as he sat cross-legged beneath a tree, gazing at Brown's dead body and listening absently to his horse cropping the short, dry grass that grew in the grove, he began to have a small regret over having brought in the Comancheros. He knew that if anyone discovered his role in that fiasco, he would die damn sudden. The very name "Comanchero" instilled a cold dread in most southwesterners. For a white man to arrange for them to attack a ranch would be considered a monstrous crime, punishable only by death.

Shivering, he rose and stared at the distant rimrock and decided man's greed was his worst vice, not because it led him to do horrible things, but because it usually wound up getting him killed.

A few miles from where Butch Hanks brooded over his uncivilized decline, Amelia Jorstad sat on the front porch of the Jorstad ranch and rocked gently back and forth, listening to the hypnotic sound of the squeaky rockers and promising to do something about them just as her brother had promised in years past.

McKiver sat on the porch rail watching the light from inside the front room flicker off her fine features and marveled at the hugeness of her eyes. He had loved her for five years now, but he was a quiet man not given to expressing himself openly. As much as he yearned for her, he could never bring himself to declare his feelings. He knew Wag Jorstad had been aware of his secret, but he also knew that the man had lived by his own strict code, which meant a man must stomp his own snakes, and if he saddled a bronc, then it was up to him to ride him. However, McKiver's love for Amelia Jorstad had been one bronc he couldn't bring himself to mount. I reckon I'm afraid of getting throwed, he thought.

Amelia nurtured a secret of her own. She, in her turn, had loved McKiver for a long time and believed he loved her. She wondered why he had never spoken and lately thought it might be that he believed Butch Hanks had won her heart and hand, and that he was on the outside track.

Looking up at him now she mused, "You know, Lud, that Butch, I just don't trust him. I don't like us finding that Hanks rider among the Comancheros. You figure he had anything to do with that raid?"

McKiver knew damn well Hanks had something to do with the raid, but he couldn't prove it, so he merely grunted, "Could be, but it would be taking a hell of a chance."

Two men came from the barn leading horses, and

McKiver and Amelia walked out in the yard. McKiver asked, "You boys riding out?"

Sharp nodded, then realizing McKiver couldn't see him in the pale light, said aloud, "Yeah. Me and Cam figured we better take us a little look-see over toward Dry Springs where those fellers picked Amelia up. Maybe Vent give 'em the slip and is hiding out there somewhere."

Sharp did not believe it for one minute. He and Spencer had decided to go and hunt up Vent's remains and see that he got a decent Christian burial, figuring they owed him at least that.

"You want some riders?" McKiver asked. "The way it looks to me, it ain't the best place for you two fellers to be wandering around in. They's still Taper riders out there. Tiny came from Jerome a little bit ago and said Grey Taper and Boots Thomas tangled horns in the Devil's Rondeevoo and Thomas won. Taper rode out without a shot being fired. He's some mad, though, 'cause Tiny found Smiley Brown layin' dead on the wagon road. He brought him on in. Reckon we'll plant him out there with the other desert garbage."

It was a long speech for McKiver, and Sharp and Spencer took it seriously but decided not to accept the use of the Jorstad riders, fearing that Hanks might decide to pull another raid.

"You keep those guards out," Sharp cautioned. "If any more of them Comancheros show up, shoot first and ask questions later."

Nodding, McKiver stood beside Amelia and watched them ride out. Five minutes later he heard the soft exchange of voices between the eastern line guard and the two men, then their hooves died away, muffled by sand and distance.

As they rode along cautiously keening the wind for

sounds alien to the desert, Spencer suddenly said, "Damn me, but that McKiver is thick-headed."

Sharp glanced around at him and laughed softly. "Some fellers have to be hit over the head by Cupid before they wake up to the fact the love bug has gnawed on their carcass."

The next morning found them camped in a small canyon, boiling coffee over a smokeless fire and waiting for the biscuits and bacon to finish cooking. Before choosing the place, they had ridden far back up the canyon, only to discover it opened out into a large valley, this one leading back to the desert.

"Well, they can't box us, anyway," Sharp observed as he dismounted and went for wood.

Now they kept a wary ear attuned to the desert, not wanting Taper's men or a stray band of Apaches to ride in on them for breakfast.

"You figure it'll take two more days to make Dry Springs?" Sharp asked, thinking, and how many days to find Vent?

"At least that, providing these horses hold up," Spencer said.

"This time we got enough water, what with six full canteens, and I put together a lot of extra grub just for you on account of the way you get on the outside of almost anything set in front of you. I bet you'd eat dog meat just like the warhoops do."

Spencer grinned. "As a matter of fact, I once did eat dog meat up north at a Sioux encampment on the Green River." Then he slowly stiffened and raised his eyes to Sharp and said in a whisper, "We got us some company. Just behind you . . ."

Spencer did not move, but instead kept on turning the bacon as Sharp walked over to a pile of wood and leaned down as if he were going to pick some up. Instead, he swept his rifle from where it rested against his saddle and, spinning on his boot heels all in an instant, fired two shots so fast Spencer never saw the lever move.

"Ah, God!" a man screamed and pitched from behind a nearby rock, his rifle clattering to the canyon floor and blood suddenly spurting from his cheek where Sharp's .38-40 slug had drilled a neat hole, erupting out the back in bone splinters and bloody froth.

When Sharp moved, Spencer moved too, drawing his Colt and slamming a shot into a bush fifty feet from their campsite. There was a brief thrashing, then a man staggered out, dropped his head on his chest, and coughed blood from his gaping mouth down over his shirt front. He began a slow topple toward the ground.

Spencer did not wait to see him hit, but instead rolled behind a large boulder near the fire and fired twice at dark shadows running along the face of the cliff opposite his position. He cursed when he saw the small rock blisters left by his missed rounds; then Sharp fired the big rifle, and a man shouted high and wild down canyon and pitched from a perch fifty feet up the cliff face to land soddenly in the sand of the canyon bottom. He did not move.

Sharp joined Spencer behind the rock, and as the two looked around for another target, a flurry of shots smashed at them from across the canyon where a small crevasse apparently hid four riflemen. As the bullets struck their fort rock, Spencer said disgustedly, "Now, we ain't gonna get to eat our food."

Sharp was more concerned about their water. The canteens were stacked near the fire and easy targets for the hidden gunmen.

"Cover me," he snapped, and springing over the rock barrier as Spencer poured shots into the crevasse, the gambler scooped up the carrying straps of the precious containers and dove back behind the boulder just ahead of half a dozen hornetlike bullets that cut the air where he had been a moment before.

Each man had a drink and then reloaded, and Sharp, knowing that if they remained here long, the mysterious attackers would eventually flank them, decided the best defense was an offense. Laying aside the rifle, he lifted his Colt free, carefully checked the loads, and said mildly, "You ready?"

Spencer replied, "Hell, no, but then, I'll never be ready," and they burst from the safety of their rock cover and ran zigzagging across the canyon floor, firing as they came. The move took the men in the crevasse completely by surprise, and Sharp whipped into the entrance and, sixgun held at hip level, blasted until he ran out of shells, then dove clear while Spencer finished the job, cutting the two remaining men down in a hail of lead.

As they ducked back inside the crevasse, both men quickly scooped up one of the fallen gunmen's pistols and turned just as three tough-looking riders came pelting across the canyon, apparently figuring to catch Sharp and Spencer reloading. It was a fatal error.

Stepping clear of the crevasse, the two opened up and, as the black powder smoke boiled around them, cold-bloodedly shot all three men off their feet.

As suddenly as it had started, it stopped, and an eerie silence took possession of the canyon as gunshot echoes faded off up the canyon to bounce from bend to bend and finally end somewhere at the other side of the rimrock.

Looking dazed, Spencer asked, "How the hell did we manage to survive that?"

"Luck, I guess," Sharp said, then walked to the camp and pulled off his coat.

Spencer, seeing blood on Sharp's shoulder, hurried forward and, turning him, asked, "Bad?"

"Feels like my shoulder's gone. Reckon no bones are busted . . . still move my arm," Sharp said, suiting action to words.

"Left shoulder," Spencer observed as he tore away the cloth of the gambler's white shirt and used it to wipe away the blood. "Clean hole. Looks like it went through." He turned Sharp around and pulled the rest of his shirt off, examining the lower left side.

"Well, I'll be damned," he exclaimed as he reached out and removed a battered chunk of lead that was clinging to Sharp's side, held there by the sticky blood that oozed from the exit hole.

"Sit down," Spencer ordered. Then he brought one of the canteens to the gambler, allowed him a drink, and began cleaning up the wounds. Once the wounds were clean and the water had sloshed away any dust that may have settled on them, Spencer used what was left of Sharp's shirt to apply a crude bandage.

"I got another shirt in my saddlebags," Sharp said and, when Spencer brought it, struggled into it with the ex-foreman's help.

While Sharp sat on the rock and puffed at one of his inevitable cigars, Spencer walked among the dead, checking to see if any of them rang a memory bell. None did but he found one man still alive, and when he bent to check him, the badly wounded cowboy opened his eyes and murmured, "Water." Sharp got up and, carrying a canteen in his good right hand, walked over and knelt beside Spencer. Taking a long drink he asked conversationally, "Who you working for?"

"Water," the man begged. Sharp took another drink, this time deliberately allowing a small trickle of the fluid to run down his chin.

"Who you work for?" he asked again.

Eyes filled with hate, the rider said hoarsely, "Hanks. We work for Butch Hanks, damn his soul to hell."

"Mad at him, are you?" Sharp asked, blowing smoke at the man.

Turning his head to one side he said, "You promised. Water."

Sighing, Sharp allowed the man a small drink then asked again, "You mad at Hanks?"

"We had it made . . . Until he decided to take over the Jorstad place . . . Crazy . . . wants everything he sees . . . gets folks killed . . . damn him," he wheezed, and his head slipped sideways into the dirt as his final breath escaped with a soft whistling sound.

Spencer gazed down at the dead man, then looked around and shook his head. "Why the hell pick on us?" he asked.

Walking toward the campfire, Sharp said over his shoulder, "They made a deal. Hanks and Taper. Let's eat." He sat cross-legged by the fire and filled a tin plate with bacon and two biscuits, poured a cup of coffee, and fell to.

Spencer joined him, and the two men sat and chewed their food reflectively while occasionally glancing around at the dead bodies that littered the canyon floor. Finally Spencer asked, "Where the hell did you learn to use a gun the way you do?"

"I was sorta teethed on a handgun. Learned to use one of the damn things when I was just a kid back in Texas. Then I found out I was a pretty fair gambler. Had to get better than fair at using a gun or wind up on the floor of some honky-tonk with a slug in my brisket. I got me a handgun and loaded up a pack mule. Rode way to hell and gone out in the desert and then just drifted. I kept working on my draw until I had her down pretty pat . . ."

"Damn wonder some Injun didn't lift yer hair," Spencer said.

"I saw 'em, lots of 'em. Only tangled with them once in over a year, and by that time I had gotten damn good. Killed five so quick it took my breath away . . . Scared the hell outta me that I could be that fast."

"You faster than Leatherhand?" Spencer asked curiously.

"No, and neither is any other man I ever saw use a gun," Sharp said positively. "I've watched Wyatt Earp, Doc Holliday, Wes Hardin, Ben Thompson, and even old Wild Bill, and with the exception of Hickok, I don't reckon they's a man among the lot who can beat Torrey."

"That good, huh?"

"That Mex, Cholo? He was some fast, snake fast. Leatherhand killed him with his gun still in leather, so McKiver told me."

"You must know this here country pretty well," Spencer said, laying his empty plate to one side and rolling a cigarette.

Tossing his plate on top of Spencer's, Sharp dug out a cigar, lit it, and said, "Yep, I been north clean up into the Green River country and even rode all the way to the Musselshell River in Montana Territory. I've seen cave houses where Injuns once lived, and them places was as big as any white man ever built and just as modern.

"Once, over near the San Carlos Reservation, I almost stepped on a snake that was as orange as a sunset . . ."

"Fer a man who loves the outdoors you picked a peculiar calling," Spencer observed, standing up and beginning to clean up the campsite.

"Well, I reckon a man does what he's good at," Sharp said, and he went to his horse and, using his good arm, tightened the cinch and adjusted his bedroll. Then he looked over his shoulder at Spencer and added, "Besides, I'm a feller who enjoys the finer things of life. I like the feel of good clothes and fine linens. I take my pleasures from sitting down to a roast duck dinner across the table from a beautiful woman, knowing that before the night's over, I'm gonna get my saddle horn polished."

Spencer grinned, then fastened the camping gear behind his cantleboard and sheathed his Winchester. Mounting, he rode out into the middle of the canyon and looked around. Then he dismounted and went from man to man removing gunbelts and picking up rifles. Tying the rifles in a tight bundle, he fastened them behind Sharp's cantleboard and hung the gunbelts from his own saddlehorn.

"I reckon their horses will be down canyon," Sharp said. "You figure they's a man guarding them?"

"Probably," Spencer said, and they each took a side of the canyon and rode cautiously toward the desert floor, eyes alert and darting from rock to rock and bush to bush.

Half an hour put them near the mouth of the canyon, where a dozen horses stood with heads hanging down in the blistering heat. As they cake walked their horses forward, nothing stirred, but Sharp had an eerie feeling they were being watched, and letting his eyes drift to his right, he caught just a glimpse of something shining on metal. Dropping off the left side of his horse like a stone, he said, "Down!" and palmed his gun as he crouched behind the animal.

Sharp had acted immediately, dismounting in one fluid motion as a shot slammed from behind a boulder, its muzzle blast blowing dust in the air from beneath its barrel.

Spencer fired twice very rapidly, then jerked his rifle from the scabbard and ran south as Sharp laid down a vicious covering fire.

Once Spencer was under cover, Sharp pulled his own rifle free and, using the horse for cover, backed toward the cliff and a pile of boulders while Spencer pumped shots toward the hidden gunman. His third slug struck the top of the rock hiding the rifleman, bounced upward, catching the rifle neatly under the barrel, and hurled it end over end. There was a yelp, then scuffling noises, followed by the sudden staccato beat of running hooves.

"Damn," Sharp cried and ran up canyon, lifted his rifle, then suddenly held his fire, gaping in amazement.

When he didn't shoot, Spencer yelled, "What's the matter?"

Shaking his head, the gambler returned to the horses. He stopped short and walked behind a bush, looked down, then waved a hand at Spencer, who joined him there.

Lying on his face in the sand was the almost naked body of a man, a thin vine wrapped neatly around his neck and deeply embedded in the flesh of his throat.

"What the hell did you see up there?" Spencer asked again, staring down at the dead man in amazement.

"A damned Injun, an Apache. He was stark naked except for a gunbelt and a rag tied around his head. He was riding one of these feller's horses. Probably killed this here gent and was fixing to take off with the other horses when we showed up."

Two hours later they were moving steadily east. Spencer had begun to worry about Sharp. Looking back several times he had noticed the gambler sway in the saddle then catch himself, and he was getting even paler than his usual saloon complexion. They had decided against wasting time trying to find Vent, figuring that if he managed to survive he probably was a long way from where they had last heard of him. If he was dead, he'd wait a little longer.

Pulling up, Spencer allowed Sharp to catch him. He held his horse in and said, "You feel all right, partner?"

"No, not really, but then, I don't guess I got me any other choice, unless you can suggest something."

Spencer grinned. "Well, I was thinking we'd stop off at the hospital just up around the bend and get that arm fixed, then sleep for twenty-four hours."

"Good idea," Sharp said and, dropping his chin on his chest, rode along stolidly. Spencer wasn't sure whether the gambler was asleep and staying in the saddle by instinct or if he was awake and just resting his eyes against the bitter glare of the sun.

Pulling up, he unlashed a canteen, and when Sharp's horse stopped too, he nudged the gambler and said, "Sorry to wake you, but you better have a drink before you dry up and just naturally blow away," and handed him the canteen.

Sharp had his drink and they pushed on. Later, Spencer was to say the trip was one of the toughest he had ever had to endure. "It's one thing to ride across a hundred miles of desert when you're in good health, but it sure as hell's another when you got a partner who's falling out of the saddle every five miles."

On the third day, Spencer and Sharp sat their horses five miles out in the desert and watched the lights go on by twos and threes in the distant town of Dry Springs.

"Where do we go from here?" Sharp asked weakly, and Spencer knew that if he didn't get the gambler in a bed soon he would die. Sharp had a lot of hard bark on him, Spencer knew, but even his great strength had limits. No man could be expected to carry a bullet hole in him for three days through a desert where the heat during the day would break a thermometer and during the night freeze the mercury in one. He turned his horse north, and Sharp's black followed. Spencer had seriously considered bringing the Hanks' mounts along with them as proof of the man's complicity in a murder attempt, but then wondered who the hell he would show them to. In the end they elected to off-saddle the animals and turn them loose to either be picked up by Apaches or find their way home.

Now he was glad they didn't have the extra horses to consider. It was going to be enough of a problem taking care of Sharp.

A short ride north and Spencer turned into a small valley, riding close to a rock wall on the east side of it, warily staring ahead as if he expected an ambush. When he saw a light gleaming forth from a small cabin nestled between two huge boulders, he rode boldly in and dismounted. Walking around to Sharp, he helped him off the black and up a set of wooden steps to a small veranda. Knocking on a door fronting the yard he waited, supporting Sharp against the wall.

Inside the cabin, May jerked open the double-barreled shotgun she kept in a corner, checked the loads, grunted with satisfaction, and looked at Vent, who was sitting at the table eating a bowl of beef stew and sopping up the juice with a biscuit. Lifting his gun free, he laid the .44 on the table by his hand and nodded.

May went to the door and asked sharply, "Who's there?"

"It's me, May . . . Spencer. Open up, dammit. I got Sharp out here and he's been shot."

"Let 'em in," Vent said, but he kept his hand near his gun.

Throwing open the door, May lifted the shotgun and leveled the gaping bores at Spencer's head, then seeing Sharp tilted against the wall, a great bloody bandage around his chest, she immediately lowered the weapon and said, "Bring him in and put him on that bed." Laying aside the shotgun, she helped Spencer move the gambler across the room. Halfway there Spencer looked up and saw Vent, who had gone back to eating, and exclaimed, "Damn ghost. I must be hallucinating. Too much sun."

May pushed a wisp of hair from her eyes and said, "When he came through that door, he was in worse shape than your gambler friend there," then bent over Sharp and began removing the bandage. "Get some water from the kettle on the stove," she ordered, and Spencer, throwing curious glances at Vent as he crossed the room, filled a washbasin and brought it back and placed it on the bedstand. Stripping away the bloody cloth and drawing a yelp from Sharp in the doing, May bared the wound and had her look.

"A little infection. Not bad," she observed, as if talking to herself. "In that chest of drawers. A wooden box. Got some doctorin' stuff in it. Alcohol, bandages, stuff a young army doc left here once," she said and grinned humorlessly as if she had just recalled something.

Spencer found the box and brought it to the bed, then went and sat down at the table and asked, "You eat all that or is there some left?"

"On the stove," May said over her shoulder. "Help yourself, but first you better put them horses in the back corral. I get visitors out here, ya know."

Spencer, his face reddening, rose, mumbled something, and left. Vent walked over and, bending down, had his look at Sharp's wound. "You'll live," he observed and went back to the table.

Sharp turned his head and asked weakly, "You don't happen to have some drinkin' likker around here, do you?"

"On the shelf," May said and pulled a bandage around the gambler's chest as he flinched in pain. "Sorry," she told him, and her voice softened as she looked at his suddenly white face.

Vent brought the whiskey and helped Sharp sit up and take his drink, then left the bottle on the bedstand and went outside, picking up his pistol as he passed the table.

After he left, May said, "That feller, he somehow gives me a funny feeling. It's almost as if he makes me ashamed of what I do for a living. He don't say nothin', but I get the feeling . . . Hell, I even offered to polish his saddle horn for nothing. Turned me down very polite like . . . Guess his kind just don't go with my kind."

Sharp lifted a hand and laid it against her cheek and said, "You gotta understand men like Torrey. They can't afford to let down their guard a minute. Life for them can be damn sudden, so can death."

Vent and Spencer came in then, and Spencer dropped his bedroll in a corner and, looking at May, asked quietly, "You mind a couple more star boarders, May?"

She sighed. "What the hell. I needed a rest anyway. Sure, but you fellers are gonna have to stay outta sight. I never know who's gonna show up around here."

"Thanks," Spencer said simply, then dropped on his bedroll and went immediately to sleep.

Chapter VI

The three men remained hidden at the lonely shack in the rocky canyon for three weeks while Sharp slowly mended and Vent gained back his lost weight. For several days a fever raged through the gambler's body, then it broke, leaving him weak and spent. Three times while the men sat silently watching the door, May had visitors, and three times she sent them away, explaining that a relative from back East was visiting and she was closed for business. Once during Sharp's convalescence, Harp Sinclair came to the cabin, and May gave him a list of groceries and money Vent had insisted she accept, and he went away and came back the next day with a wagon. Sitting up on the front seat with the saloon owner was Carl Shipley, a Winchester across his lap and a heavy old six-shooter dangling from a cutaway dragoon holster at his belt.

Pulling in the team in front of the cabin, he grinned up at May and said, "Hear tell you're taking strays. Got room for a couple more?"

"Come up, you two. I'm just about ready to dish up the last of the stew, and, boys, my stew's famous from here to the Canadian line," she said.

As she started back into the cabin, Sinclair grinned

and observed, "That ain't the only thing that's famous from here to Canada."

May ignored him. The visitors packed in the groceries and found Vent and his two companions playing poker at the kitchen table with matches. A fourth place, apparently May's position at the table, had most of the matches piled up in front of a hand of cards she had placed facedown. Looking at the matches, Sinclair observed dryly, "I bet you fellers a plug of Day's Work terbaccy I kin name the top player in this here game."

Nobody accepted the bet. Sharp looked disgusted, noting sourly, "Women should stick to what they're best at."

May came and put an arm around the gambler's neck and, kissing him on the cheek, said, "Anytime, handsome, anytime."

Spencer, apparently embarrassed by the blond woman's show of affection, rose and went outside. Vent got up and followed him, and in a few moments the other men came out and sat around on the veranda in the light breeze that had somehow found this desolate canyon. Sinclair originally purchased it because it had one of the few springs in the area. The water was ice cold and came straight from a cut in the rocks, probably traveling underground for miles.

Vent eased down into an old rocking chair, adjusted the .44, and, lifting his boot heels to the veranda rail, said casually, "Nice evening for a fire, don't you think, boys?"

Sinclair looked at him sharply. "A fire?"

"I was kinda thinking along those lines. Maybe burn down a house and barn and a few outbuildings over to the D-Ring-T?"

Spencer grinned. "Now, that ain't a half-bad notion," he said, looking at Sharp, who was cleaning his pistol, head down and eyes paying close attention to what he was doing. "What you think, Owney?" he asked.

Sharp looked up and stared off toward the west, where the sun was just starting to tip over the horizon, and observed, "Nothing like a good hot fire to give a man a taste of what hell's gonna be like."

"You fellers are asking for a neck-stretching," Shipley protested.

"Maybe not," Sinclair said. "Tonight Grey and his boys will be at my place gettin' likkered up. He brings 'em to town about twice a week and they try to drink my place dry. They'd be nothing more than a couple of horse guards out there tonight."

Vent stood up and looked south where the D-Ring-T lay in the center of Taper's cattle empire and mused, "A man without a house is a man with nothin' left but another feller's land. All the ground Grey Taper owns is one section where his house sits. The rest belongs to the government. He holds it as long as he has the guns. When they go, he becomes nothing more than a homesteader with thirty thousand head of cattle running loose for the grabbing."

Sharp stared at him as did the others. "Hell, I never did think on it that way," Sinclair said, "But Vent's damn sure right. Taper don't own the ground his cattle run on, that's for sure. In fact, they ain't a rancher in Arizona who actually owns his land. They use government land and hold it against nesters and other folks because they got more guns and don't have any problem with bumping over a feller or two."

"So, I guess maybe tonight I'll just wander over that way and see if I can't get old Grey usta sleeping on the ground again," Vent said. "Hell, he's always braggin' about how he came into this country with nothin' but a horse, saddle, and bedroll, and fit Injuns and outlaws and slept on the ground until he grew big enough to build. Reckon he won't mind doing it again, seeing as how he's kinda familiar with it."

"Want some company?" Spencer asked.

"Thanks," Vent said.

Sharp finished wiping the excess oil from his gun, making certain the butt plates were completely dry so they wouldn't slip in his hand, then, holstering the gun, he rose and walked over and leaned on the rail with his back to the yard. He had his look at the others and said mildly, "I'll go along," and went back inside. A few minutes later he stuck his head back out and called the men to supper.

Five dusty riders, their clothes shedding the fine powder of the desert, tied their horses to the hitchrail in front of the Red Horse Saloon beside a dozen more carrying the same brand. It didn't take a pair of glasses to see the large D-Ring-T brand on the left flank of each of the animals as they stood hipshot at the rail and waited patiently for their riders to finish their carousing.

Slapping the dust from their chaps with their hats, the men tramped inside and were greeted by calls to "belly up to the bar and wet yer whistle," which the five proceeded to do. After they had been served, one man, the apparent leader of the rest, turned and looked toward a table near the back wall where Grey Taper sat. At the table was Cole Butram, the quiet Shorty Hodge, loud-talking Tuck Willoby, and Vance Caudell, a tall, deadly-eyed Missourian who men said fought with Quantrell during the War Between the States. He wore two guns on a single cartridge belt without holsters. Instead a screw in the side of the pistol fit in a metal notch fastened to the belt, allowing the user to spin the weapon up and bang away without wasting time on the draw. It was a good system as long as your target stood his ground directly in front of you, but if he decided to move around, the hipshooter then found himself spinning around like a whirling dervish in his attempt to keep the other fellow within range. The end result of all this was that the man with the hip guns usually wound up in an early grave if he had a bent toward violence.

The newly arrived rider facing the room nodded at Taper and said, "We found nothing, Mr. Taper. If he's out there he's dead. No man could survive that long in that hellhole, no man."

Taper glared. "Bring me his body and I'll believe you."

Near the front end of the bar a short, stocky man with a beard who was dressed rather nondescriptly raised his head and glanced toward Taper, had his long look, and turned away. The gesture was not missed by Butram, who nudged Hodge in the ribs and asked low-voiced, "You know that feller at the end of the plank?"

Hodge glanced casually at him then shook his head. "Never seen that waddy. Why?"

"He was sure as hell giving the boss the once over," Butram told him.

"Well, maybe he's just the curious type," Hodge said. "Hell, the man's drinking. He ain't bothered anyone. Ain't no law agin' looking at somebody."

"They just might be if we don't know him," Butram argued.

Realizing the unfruitful search for Vent Torrey was beginning to get on the new foreman's nerves, Hodge figured Butram was probably just on the prod and that he'd settle down, but he was wrong. Instead, he rose suddenly and walked down the room, and as Hodge and Taper, who had looked up when Butram left the table, watched, stopped five feet from the stranger. Bowing his head, he said sharply, "Mister, you seem awful damn interested in my boss. Why?"

The short, bearded stranger turned easily and, placing his back to the bar, said, "What? What's the problem?"

Angry now, Butram asked sharply, "I said, why you staring at Mr. Taper?"

"Just curious. Wondered if I had ever seen his face on a wanted dodger," the stranger said.

Taper rose then and walked over and looked at the man. "Why would you think I might be wanted somewhere, feller?" he asked.

"Old habit of mine," the stranger said.

Butram turned and looked at Taper, then asked, "You want a better answer outta this pilgrim, Mr. Taper?"

While Butram was talking, the stranger had his look at the foreman, then asked Taper, "This feller your ramrod?"

"He's my foreman," Taper said, and now he wondered about this odd little man. It was obvious there wasn't a grain of fear in him. It was almost as if he knew he had the upper hand. Taper didn't like it. The man made him uneasy.

"Then you put a dog line on him or you're gonna have to find you a new foreman," the stranger said, and his eyes were very, very cold.

At that moment the batwings swung open and four riders came in. They were tall men, and each wore his gun as if he knew how to use it. Looking them over Taper realized he was seeing fighting men, not just cowboys. One of the newcomers, taking in the scene at a sweeping glance, made a quick motion with one hand and the three men with him spread out along the wall. Quickly glancing at them, Taper realized they were now standing in deep shadow. He did not like the way this was shaping up. The last thing he wanted now was a fight with a strange outfit.

The fourth rider asked quietly, "Any problems, Mr. Slaughter?" and several men around the room sucked in their breath and let their hands move clear of their weapons.

Taper also was taken aback. He had almost pushed his men into a fight with the legendary Texas John Slaughter, a lawman whose reputation for deadly fighting skills coupled with phenomenal luck was known all over the Southwest. His men were almost as famous, for he hired only ex-lawmen and ex-rangers. Taper had heard recently that this quiet little man had just been asked to become sheriff of Cochise County, home of Tombstone, labeled long ago as the town too tough to die.

Butram, having crowded himself into a crack, now knew that if anybody busted a cap, he would die very sudden. He held no aspirations of being able to beat John Slaughter to the draw.

Taper took Butram by the arm and said cordially, "Sorry, Mr. Slaughter, but of course you are welcome to our town, as your men are. It's just that we've had a little trouble here abouts; a gunman killed my son right out there in the street. We're nervous about strangers."

"Fine, then my men will have a drink and I'll have another and we'll move on. We've got a lot of miles between us and Texas," Slaughter said.

"You returning to Texas?" Taper asked.

Picking up his drink Slaughter nodded at Sinclair and said mildly, "Give my boys a jug and some glasses," and then, looking at Taper, added, "I'm planning on bringing four thousand head of cattle to Tombstone."

"Jesus, that's a hell of a lot of cattle, sir," Taper observed as Butram, forgotten, returned to his seat at the table and poured himself a drink with hands that shook. Behind him Vance Caudell grinned slightly.

"A lot of cattle," Slaughter agreed. "Who was the shooter who killed your boy?" The little lawman glanced up and looked directly into Taper's eyes.

"Feller by the name of Vent Torrey. Some call him Leatherhand. Wears a funny contraption on his gun-hand. Fast as billy hell . . ."

"You say he plugged your boy?"

Taper nodded. "Yep, right out there in the street. Didn't give the kid a chance. Shot him down."

"Funny thing for Torrey to pull. I knew him when he was over in Colorado. Damn good lawman. Respected by everybody. Has friends all up and down the front range. Some say Doc Holliday's a close friend. Seems Doc patched Torrey up once, and they been friends ever since."

"Never heard that," Taper said, and the cold, gray-eyed face of the infamous Holliday drifted into his mind's eye. He had heard a lot of stories about the deadly dentist, and all of them were bad. Holliday killed without mercy and for almost nothing. He also hated cattlemen and cowboys, as did Wyatt Earp and his brothers. Thinking about it he suddenly realized that Earp, Holliday, and the rest of their bunch were even now in Tombstone. Earp was marshal and Doc ran a poker table there.

"Doc, he ain't a feller to forget a friend," Slaughter observed, watching Taper's face. It was obvious the big man did not like what he was hearing, and it was also obvious he did not want Slaughter to know it.

"Tell me something, Mr. Slaughter. Why is it everywhere this feller Leatherhand goes he has friends?"

Slaughter shrugged. "Some men are just that way. I reckon in Torrey's case most men know him as a man who keeps his word and a man who more than once has risked his life for someone else, or stuck out his neck to help a friend . . . I'm not saying your boy made the mistake in this thing 'cause I wasn't there, Mr. Taper, but if I was you I'd do my best to learn a bit more about that shooting."

Taper shook his head. "I'm satisfied. I don't give a damn how many friends this jasper has. If he still lives, I'll hang him to the oak tree in my front yard. If he's dead out there in the desert, my boys will bring me his guns and his bones."

"And what happens when it's all over, Mr. Taper? I have to tell you that the Bowdrey shooting has traveled from one end of this state to the other. D-Ring-T is already considered outlawed. Bowdrey was a good man, and he deserved more than he got. Many of us called him friend." Slaughter turned and nodded at his men and left the saloon.

Taper returned to his table, and when Butram would have spoken to him, snarled, "The next time you get a case of the braveries, I'm gonna let you ride whatever bronc you saddle," and he filled his glass and drank deep, hating what was happening to him but unable to stop it.

Taper drank steadily, his face closed and tight with his thoughts. His men stayed away from him. They had had experience in the past with Grey Taper on a brooding drunk. In that condition he had killed men. No one wanted to rile him now.

Shoe Slocum did not know this. He swamped out the saloon, the Jinglebob Cafe and cleaned stable for old Pegleg Harley Cates, the one-legged livery owner. Now he slid into a chair opposite Taper, and pushing his battered hat back on his head, stared at the ranch owner.

Looking up, Taper said shortly, "Get away from here, swamper. You smell like shit."

"You'd smell that way too if all ya did all day was clean up other folks' leavins'," Shoe said, but he did not move.

Taper, his face red now, glanced at Tuck Willoby and said harshly, "Tuck, turn this thing into a steer for me, will ya," and Willoby, grinning, drew a huge Bowie knife and started around the table.

Shoe looked at him, then said, "You do that and you ain't gonna find out where that Leatherhand feller is hidin'."

Willoby stopped and looked at Taper, who was suddenly stone sober. "What did you say?" Taper asked.

"I know where that gunfighter and his friends are holed up," Shoe said.

"You tell me," Taper ordered, his voice hoarse with anticipation.

Shoe held up a hand and said, "First, you call off this feller with the pig sticker, then you come up with some coin and we talk," and it was obvious Shoe was enjoying keeping Taper in suspense.

Taper surprised him. Nodding at Willoby he picked up his drink and faced the bar, ignoring the swamper.

"And now, little man . . ." Willoby said as he reached a long arm across the edge of the table and grasped Shoe by the throat, cutting him off in mid-squeal. Nobody at the bar paid any attention. Somebody was always hoorawing the swamper, but they never hurt him, so nobody bothered to interfere now as Willoby's knife flicked downward, neatly severing Shoe's waist band and slicing through the rope he wore for a belt at the same time. Another swift knife stroke and the pants separated at the hip.

"Hey now, you wait now, hey," Shoe protested through his partially constricted throat.

Willoby ignored him. He continued cutting cloth until Shoe found himself sitting there in little more than rags.

Eyes bulging, the swamper gasped out, "I'll . . . tell ya . . . I'll tell ya," and Willoby released him and stood by with the knife resting on Shoe's shoulder, the blade inches from his unprotected throat, and waited.

Only then did Taper look at him. "Now, swamper, where?"

"They's out at May's cabin," he said.

"The whore's?" Taper asked.

"Yes . . . They's at the whore's cabin. Been there quite a while now . . ."

Nodding at Willoby, who sheathed his knife and returned to his seat grinning faintly, Taper dug in his pocket and came up with fifty dollars in gold. Tossing it to the swamper, he said casually, "Here, buy yourself some new clothes, and while you're at it, take a bath. Now get out of here."

Snatching up the gold, Shoe ducked out a side door, looking for all the world like a human scarecrow the birds had attacked.

Standing up, Taper turned to Butram and said sharply, "Bring the boys. We ride." Then he went out to his horse, carrying the half-empty whiskey jug in his left hand and a glass in his right. As he stood swaying on the sidewalk, he drank the glass dry, then hurled it high in the air, and, drawing his gun, fired. The glass erupted in mid-fall and Taper chuckled. As the pieces clattered into the street, Butram burst through the batwings, gun in hand, followed by several D-Ring-T riders, who also held handguns at the ready.

Looking around at them, Taper grinned widely and said, "We're going after Leatherhand, boys, mount up."

As the small army rode beneath the livery stable overhang, Shoe peered from his sleeping place in the hay and thought, I hope that gunfighter plugs you, you dirty bastard.

An hour later the riders cautiously approached the cabin in the canyon. Half a mile from it Taper held them up and sent Butram and Caudell on ahead to look around. They returned in half an hour and Caudell told Taper, "Nobody but that whore there now, Mr. Taper, but they's been several horses kept in that corral for close to a month."

"A month, huh?" Taper mused. "Just about when Torrey disappeared. Let's ride on up there and have a little powwow with old May," he said and led the men into the canyon and up to the cabin.

"Bring her out of there," he ordered Butram, and the foreman pointed at Willoby and Caudell and jerked his head, then moved up the steps to the veranda as they followed.

Tapping on the door, Butram called, "May, you there?"

"I'm here," she said, and by the sound of her voice, Butram figured she was just on the other side of the door. He was not about to go barging in, for May's shotgun was widely known and discussed around Dry Springs. Those discussions never covered even the faint possibility that she might not use the weapon if she were riled enough. Butram had seen what double-ought buckshot could do to a man.

"Want to have a little talk with you, May," Butram said.

"Who's with you?" May asked suspiciously.

"Mr. Taper's out here. He wants to talk to you, May," Butram called.

There was a long hesitation, during which Taper grew more and more restless, then she stepped through the door carrying the shotgun. Butram smiled and said, "Hell, ma'am, you don't need that," and suddenly ripped it from her grasp and threw it out near the corral, spooking May's two horses.

"Damn you, Cole Butram," May said savagely, then she rounded on Taper and, pointing a long finger at him, shouted, "So, now you ain't satisfied with bullying all the folks around Dry Springs, you gotta come out here and pick on me . . . Shame, shame . . ."

Staring at her coldly, Taper said, "Shut her stinking mouth," and watched while Butram and Willoby grabbed her and jerked her head back, cutting off any further sounds.

"Now, whore, listen to me. You had some men here for several days. Who were they and where did they go?" Taper growled and tilted the whiskey bottle and drank deep.

Watching him May was suddenly afraid. She had heard of some of the things this man was supposed to have done while drunk and they were enough to intimidate a stoic Indian. One tale had it that Taper, while deep in his cups, once ordered a cow thief wrapped in a wet cowhide then placed in the direct rays of the sun. As the hide slowly shrank, crushing the man to death by inches, Taper was supposed to have sat on a nearby rock and calmly drank from a jug.

"Yes, they were here. That gunman, Leatherhand and your foreman, Spencer. Then they was that feller who always dresses in black, that gambler feller," May blurted out. She knew Vent and his friends had no intention of returning to the cabin after this night's work was done, and she was also fully aware that someone must have tipped off Taper for him to be here now. They had read the sign in the corral, she was sure, so they knew a group of men had stayed with her for a certain length of time. By talking, she hoped to at least buy her life. She had no illusions about Grey Taper. She knew that if he so decided, he would order her hanged and be damned to what the world thought.

Now he looked down at her and asked sharply, "Where they headin'?"

"They said they was going to Jerome, but they could of been storying me," she said. "They didn't tell me much, and they never talked around me."

"Why keep them here?" Butram asked, staring at her suspiciously.

"Money," May said simply. "I'm sure Mr. Taper can understand that."

"Keep a civil tongue in your damned head or you won't have one very long," Taper snapped, then looking at the cabin, said, "you got any mementos in there you want to keep?"

Knowing now what Taper planned, she sighed and said, "Yes, a couple."

"Then get 'em," Taper ordered and, jerking a thumb toward the corrals, told Shorty Hodge, "saddle her horses and bring them around here."

May, back straight and head high, went in the cabin and, kneeling, pried up a board on the floor and removed a small carpetbag. Opening it, she looked at the contents and smiled. The bag was full of money, and lying on top of the bills was a derringer and a box of .44 shells for it. Who needed the damn cabin as long as she had this, she thought and, going to the bedstand, removed a picture of her mother and placed it on top of the pistol. Glancing around the cabin, she was amazed to see there wasn't another damn thing there she wanted to bother with. She walked to the door then and, turning, had her last look, eyes lingering on the bed the longest. Smiling at a secret thought, she walked down the steps and, while Hodge held her horse, mounted and sat stolidly staring at the cabin.

"Burn it," Taper commanded.

Caudell walked up the steps and inside, and then the sound of shattering glass was followed by an eruption of flame as the coal oil from the lamp went up. The tall Missourian came to the veranda and, standing limned against the backdrop of the burning cabin, said, "It's done, Mr. Taper."

"Then let's ride," Taper said and led them from that place at a gallop.

May did not look back.

When they reached Dry Springs several people were out on the street staring north and Taper pulled in his horse. "A cabin caught fire north of here. Nobody hurt. Go home," he barked and watched coldly as the townsmen left the street. Harp Sinclair, standing on the saloon steps, stared at May, who smiled slightly and solemnly winked, then looked away.

Taper glanced around at May and said, "I'll pay you forty dollars each for them horses and another twenty-five for the gear." Tolling out one of the riders, he jerked his thumb toward the livery and said, "Take the horses down there for now and then stay with this woman until the stage comes in the morning. Put her aboard."

Reaching in his pocket, he dug out a handful of coins. He sorted out $130, and, riding alongside May, handed it to her.

"Thanks," she said, not ungraciously.

"You know what the alternative could have been, don't you?" Taper asked.

"I know," May said and followed the rider toward the livery, thinking, he'll find out what happened to Torrey when his own damn place goes up, and he'll come for me. With that thought she knew she must run.

When they reached the barn, the rider unsaddled the horses and put them away while May stood, carpetbag at her feet, and watched. When he had finished, he turned and said, "Maybe you'd like to earn a little something while you're waiting," and watched her face.

"Maybe," she answered, waiting for his next move.

"I got me a friend who owns a 'dobe just west of Main and he ain't home now. He went to Denver on business. Said I could use his place while he was gone . . . all right?"

Shrugging, she said, "All right," and followed him outside and along the street to an alley, where he turned off and, after a few minutes' walk, stopped at a low adobe house and opened the door, standing aside for her to enter. As she stood just inside the door, she felt him brush past her, then a match flared and was touched to a lamp and the room was flooded with a dull light as he said, "Close the door."

He did not wait but immediately began shedding his clothes. May watched him for a moment then, sighing, shrugged out of her dress and underthings and went to the bed where he was already waiting and slid beneath the blankets. Half an hour later, the cowboy, his face still and serene, was snoring against her shoulder. Slipping quietly from the bed, she dressed quickly, stopping and standing half in and half out of her underskirt when he snorted and rolled over; but then he was still again, and she finished dressing, left the adobe, and walked hurriedly toward the Jinglebob Cafe.

Stumbling down an alley, she found the back door and knocked, waited and knocked again. Then a sleepy voice challenged her. "Who the hell's that?"

"It's me, May," she called in a hushed voice. "Open up, Carl."

The door swung back, revealing Shipley standing in his long handles. "What's goin' on?" he asked, peering beyond her into the alley.

"Taper burned me out tonight. Now he's on his way back to the D-Ring-T," she said, closing the door. "When he finds his place in ashes, he'll be coming back for me. I gotta leave tonight, but he forced me to sell my horses to him. If I take one of them, he'll have me arrested as a horse thief, sure as shootin'."

"I'll put you on my mare. She's sound as a dollar and can outrun any damn thing Taper's got on his spread," Shipley said, adding, "you wait here while I get dressed," and he went into another room and closed the door.

As May sat the restless mare, her carpetbag tied firmly on behind, three canteens of cold water and a bag of meat and bread strapped to the saddle horn, Shipley looked up and said, "May, I'm right sorry about the cabin."

"Hell, it belonged to you fellers," she said.

"All the same, they burned everything you owned."

Shrugging, May observed, "Hell, Carl, they wasn't much I owned that was worth saving. Taper did give me a chance to remove any keepsakes, as if I'd have any to save."

"You better ride," he told her.

"You sure I can't pay you for this mare?" she asked.

"Nope, I got another horse, and she never was for sale. She's the kinda horse you give to a friend." Looking up at her, he added, "You are a friend, May. Always will be. You write me. Let me know how you make out . . . and May . . ."

"What?"

Shipley hesitated, then said firmly, "Iffin you ever quit that business, you look me up. I reckon I could forget a lot of things . . . you understand?"

Smiling, she bent and quickly kissed him and said, "I'll think on that," and rode down the alley. She suddenly felt totally fulfilled. Harp Sinclair had said exactly the same thing to her earlier that evening.

When Vent and his two companions rode into the front yard of the D-Ring-T, they were challenged from the bunkhouse porch by a man sitting in an old chair with a rifle across his lap. Light from a window behind him left him totally vulnerable to anyone standing out in the dark, and so Vent just sat his horse and waited.

"Hey, that you, Mr. Taper?" the cowboy called.

"What's going on?" a second voice called from near the barn, and now Vent had the guards' locations pin-pointed.

Nodding toward the barn, he said quietly, "You wanta take him, Owney?"

The gambler nodded and rode toward the barn as the porch-sitter grumbled, "Damn waddies always comin' home drunk. Someday I'm gonna plug one of them fellers and teach 'em a lesson."

Two seconds after this speech ended, there was the sharp crack of a gun barrel striking skull bone, a grunt, and the sound of a body hitting the ground solidly.

Now the bunkhouse guard was suddenly alerted, and standing up, he walked out to the edge of the porch. Shading his eyes with his hand, he tried to penetrate the darkness enveloping the yard.

"Drop that rifle!" Vent said sharply, and the rider hesitated until he heard the snick of a hammer being pulled back, then bent and laid the rifle on the floor and moved away without being ordered to do so.

"What you fellers want?" he called, then as an afterthought, asked, "who are you?"

"Your death if you so much as wiggle your ears," Spencer said coldly.

"That you, Cam?" the rider called.

"Turk, you best go on out to the barn and see if you can help Garvis," Spencer said. "Get him away from the buildings and out in the field."

"What the hell you fellers going to do?" the man named Turk asked plaintively.

"Just do as you're told," Vent snapped and watched the man move off the porch and head for the barn. In a few minutes Sharp came back carrying an extra rifle across his saddle swell. Two gunbelts hung from his saddle horn.

Vent dismounted and walked to the front door, stood contemplating it for a moment, then deliberately lifted his boot and slammed it open. Striding inside, he lit a match, found a lamp, and fired it up, then carried it from room to room, lighting other lamps. When the house gleamed light from every window, he started at the back and smashed the first lamp, watching as flame and glass spewed onto curtains and over the carpets on the floor. When he finally emerged from the front door again, the house was a raging inferno, flames leaping fifty feet in the air.

Glancing toward the barn, Vent was in time to watch Spencer light a bundle of straw and pitch it into the hay mow and then lead his snorting horse to the center of the yard. As the flames raged up the walls of the barn, they leaped as if with a life of their own to the blacksmith roof, then to the tack room, and from there to several outbuildings and a large wooden granary.

Mounting, Vent said calmly, "Let's ride, boys," and led Spencer and Sharp south.

Taper was halfway between Dry Springs and the ranch when he saw the pillar of flame shooting toward the sky and exclaimed, "God almighty! It's the ranch." Slamming spurs into his horse, he led the race for the D-Ring-T. When they burst at a gallop into the front yard, the scene resembled the blasted remains of an artillery-shelled town, what with flames consuming the last of the barn and outbuildings and nothing remaining of the house but the adobe walls, now blackened by smoke and flame. The bunkhouse was a smoldering ruin.

Even the huge old oak tree had lost most of its limbs and was still burning. Staring at it, Taper shouted, "Some of you men get water from the well and put out those branches," and then the two guards came staggering through the smoke and ashes of the outbuildings and stopped in the yard, looked around blearily, and shook their heads.

Staring at them Taper rode over and said harshly, "Why ain't you fellers dead?"

Turk looked up at the big man on the silver-mounted saddle and asked, "What? What did you say?"

"I asked you why you're still alive?"

Staring at him, Garvis merely shook his head. Still dazed from the blow he had received from Sharp, he didn't even hear Taper's question.

Suddenly, shouting wildly, Taper screamed, "You bastards, you let those madmen burn my ranch," and he drew his .45 and, teeth bared, triggered it empty, the big slugs tearing into the two guard's bodies with solid, smacking sounds that ripped their insides apart and blew them in a tangled mess into the burnt grass of the yard. As they screamed in their death agonies, Taper snatched Butram's gun and, riding over them, fired it downward until it was empty too.

Butram stared at him, speechless. A post near the barn suddenly spurted flame as a pitch pocket caught, sending fire up the side of the wood in a long tongue, its flaring light casting Taper's face in demonic reflection.

Chapter VII

The three men had been riding for two days and had made a wide swing south from Dry Springs toward Diablo Canyon, then back north again through a wild country of pinnacle rocks and deep cuts that no man could cross, let alone three men on horseback. To their right loomed West Sunset Mt. and to their left the rugged country of the Apache where few men went and fewer returned to tell about it. Vent, like other men who had come to this country in the 1870s and '80s, had received his share of warnings and had listened to his ration of horror stories concerning this grisly place. Now, as he rode along with his handkerchief over his mouth in an effort to ward off the fine dust that the horses' hooves kicked up, he kept a careful eye on any stretch of ground that could serve as an ambush.

"Tough country, this here," Spencer said as he rode up and sided Vent.

"I'll tell ya, partner, if God was lookin' for a place to give the world an enema this is where he would stick the hose," Vent observed, and Spencer smiled behind his handkerchief-covered face.

Sharp quartered up beside them, his big stud turned almost gray with the dust clinging to his sweaty hide.

Looking up toward the sun, he seemed to sink in the saddle under the 100-degree heat. "If we had eggs, we could fry them on the rocks," he said.

That thought gave rise to another. "How's the water holding?" he asked Vent, who was carrying five extra canteens on his saddle.

"We'll make her," Vent answered, then looking down at the skinny neck of his horse, thought, If this damn knothead holds up, and wished he had the Appaloosa under him. He would get that horse back, and if a man rode him, that man would ride no other man's horse, he vowed.

As near as Vent could figure, Taper and his men were half a day behind them. Several times he contemplated stopping and laying an ambush for them, slowing them down and making them cautious. A man who feared being shot from cover was a man who tracked slowly and carefully, Vent knew, but then each time he looked at the horse he rode, he had decided against it. Spencer and Sharp were well mounted and could hold their own in a race. He could not, so he went on.

All the second day they moved north, seeing nothing but an occasional antelope, its light tan skin mottled with white, blending almost perfectly with its desert home. Once a huge jackrabbit with a black tail sprang from behind a bush just as they reached it and spooked the horses. The first day out from Dry Springs, Sharp's horse almost stepped on a rattlesnake. The men estimated it measured at least seven feet. Gila monsters crouched on boulders, their bodies rising and lowering as if they were doing pushups, their tiny tongues red darts testing the wind for danger and prey.

On the third day, they crossed the northern end of Diablo Canyon and rode onto a low hill overlooking the small desert town of Two Guns.

Sitting there looking at its mean cluster of buildings, Vent wondered why the hell anyone would build a town here. It lay on the Ft. Winslow-Flagstaff road, and as the men sat their weary horses and watched, a train pulled out from the station on the edge of town and, whistling mournfully, picked up speed on the run for the fort.

Lowering his handkerchief, Vent glanced at Sharp and asked, "Wanta go down and wash the dust out?"

Sharp grinned. "I'm outta cigars. Don't have any choice. We need water and we need grub. I reckon we can spend an hour there."

"Cam?" Vent asked, not looking at the ex-foreman.

"Why not. Hell, a man only lives once." He clucked to his horse and rode toward the weatherbeaten shacks of the desert spa.

"A man could die down there too, if we've underestimated Taper's travel time," Vent said to no one in particular.

They rode into the main street of Two Guns and pulled the horses up to a water trough in the square. Allowing them to drink their fill, they had their look at the town, and it was a mean place. There was a saloon, a livery stable just north of it, with a crude barn attached, a mercantile directly across the street, and a saddle shop near an alley down from the mercantile. A scattering of adobe buildings and weathered wooden shacks constituted the rest of Two Guns.

Looking at it, Sharp made a sour face and said, "I'll bet they ain't one silver dollar in this whole damn town," and pulled his horse away from the watering trough and rode it to a hitchrack in front of the saloon. Looking up at its false front, Sharp grinned. The place had no name, but merely proclaimed it was a saloon. As he stepped off his horse, Vent rode in beside him and said, "I'm going to the livery and see if I can make a trade for something a little better than this nag," and nodding, rode downstreet and in under the overhang of the livery barn, where he found a huge man standing over an anvil, a hot shoe clamped in a pair of tongs. As he swung a single jack high and brought it down hard, the sparks spiraled off the red hot iron and sizzled out in the dust of the floor.

Glancing around, he saw Vent sitting his horse and with a sigh leaned his hammer against the anvil and sloshed the shoe into a water pail, sending an acrid smoke toward the ceiling, accompanied by the crackling sound of suddenly cooling metal.

"What can I do for you, mister?" the blacksmith asked, staring at Vent's low-slung gun and then raising his eyes to meet the cold brown ones in the hard face.

"Looking to trade horses," Vent said.

The blacksmith walked around Vent's animal and came back and stood beside the anvil and said with a twinkle in his eye, "I see you're building a horse. At least ya got the frame up."

Vent smiled. Hooking a knee around the saddle horn, he rolled a careful cigarette and, striking a kitchen match on one of his silver-mounted spurs, held it to the tip. Blowing smoke at the horse's drooping ears, he said, "This old pony has had himself a long, hard ride. Feed him up, curry him down, and saddle him under good leather and he'll bring you a good price."

"Well, they's one thing about a horse like that one," the blacksmith observed. "Iffin he falls over dead—and I expect he will as soon as you ride outta town—I can always use him as bait for my coyote trap line."

"You got any tradin' material?"

"Get down. We'll go have us a look." The blacksmith led Vent through the barn to a corral in the rear where several horses stood switching flies in the blistering heat. Leaning on the fence, Vent had his look, then pointed a thumb at a line-backed buckskin that he thought might be able to run and had the tough, chunky frame of an animal with plenty of bottom, and asked, "That thing for sale?"

"Yep, everything on this lashup is for sale, Mr. Leatherhand, that is, except my anvil. I'd have to take a wagon clean over to Jerome to get another and I might not find one there. If that was the case, I'd have to order her from back East and wait until the train delivered it. In the meantime, I'd sit around over ta the saloon and drink up last year's earnings and wind up going hungry this year besides turning into a drunk."

Vent stared at the maker of this long speech. He had not missed the use of his nickname.

"I'm a man who is pressed for time, which gives the other feller a large advantage in a horse trade, Mr. Blacksmith, but you look like a fair and honest man, so I reckon I'll just trust you to name the deal."

The blacksmith scratched his head, and as the dust from his work fell onto his shirt front, he grinned and said, "I like a feller who shows good sense, and me, I ain't no gossip, but half an hour ago they was a gent rode in here from over ta Verde Valley, and he was backed by six hardcases. They was down at the saloon the last time I see them. You can have that buckskin for your horse and seventy-five dollars coin."

Knowing it was a generous deal, Vent said so, then dug out several gold pieces and paid the blacksmith, who went for a rope. Returning, he walked into the corral and, with a deft flip of the wrist, dropped a loop over the line-back's head and led the snorting animal out of the corral and into the barn. Vent transferred his saddle to the buckskin while the blacksmith led the worn-out Dry Springs horse back and turned it into the corral. The horse went straight for a feeding trough and began contentedly chewing hay.

Stepping up on the buckskin, Vent looked down at the blacksmith and asked, "What's your handle?"

"Big Jim Morgan." The man reached and shook hands with Vent, then said, "That feller who rode in . . . He had a waspy gent with him wearing a pair of fancy black batwings and enough hardware to scare the hell outta old Cochise. They looked like they was on the hunt or maybe just out to plug somebody to see 'em fall."

"Thanks again," Vent said and rode out.

As he rode toward the barn door, Morgan called, "I always liked Earl Bowdrey, and I never did like Branda or Grey Taper. A blacksmith hears a lot. I hear those two and a feller name of Hanks has made an Indian pact and signed a war scroll. You're the target."

Vent waved a hand and rode into the street. As he trotted the buckskin toward the saloon, he glanced around. A strange stillness pervaded the street and the buildings, and glancing back, it suddenly came to Vent that the town could have been a ghost for all the action showing. Nobody walked the street. Nobody showed inside the saddle shop or the mercantile. It was as if Morgan were the only human creature in the town.

Rounding into the hitckrack he tied the buckskin, then thought better of it and loosened all three horses and led them down an alley and around the corner behind the saloon. A corral back there held two shaggy desert ponies, probably stolen from the Indians, Vent figured, but no other life showed. He tied the horses to the corral, touching noses with the Indian ponies, and walked to a back door that stood open and, closing his eyes, stepped inside, then opened them, seeing the room clearly. He had learned that from Boots Thomas, who had explained that by this trick the eye became used to darkness and when opened could see perfectly in a room with even minimal light.

The place was empty except for Spencer and Sharp, who sat at a table near the back wall and drank beer and wolfed down *tortillas* and *frijoles*, chasing them with hot peppers.

Sliding into a chair with his back to the wall, Vent said quietly, "Branda, Hanks, and some of his men rode in here less than an hour ago. Blacksmith said they acted kinda spooky. He heard from over to Jerome, Hanks, Branda, and Taper have thrown in together."

Spencer chewed thoughtfully. Sharp wiped his mouth with a napkin, sighed, and lit a cigar. Leaning back in his chair, he said, "An' the condemned hombre chomped down a hearty last meal."

Pointing at the *frijoles*, Spencer said, "Better fill up while you can, friend. May be your last chance."

Vent filled a plate and motioned to the bartender, a fat man with shoe-button eyes, a rolling seaman's walk, and a closed expression on his face, and he came over and set a glass of beer in front of him and warned, "The stuff is hot, it tastes like horse piss and it's green as the grass on the plains, but you'll get used to it. It's all I got, unless ya want whiskey."

Sharp looked up at him and asked, "Who makes your whiskey?"

"Feller lives just west of here on the railroad line. Does some gandy-dance work for the track master and kinda uses his extra time to cook up sour mash whiskey."

"He any good?" Vent asked. In his part of Missouri most of the whiskey was homemade and highly regarded by the locals.

"Pretty damn good unless he gets to sampling his stuff, then it kinda tastes funny. I accused him once of putting chewing tobacco in it and he denied it."

Sharp held up a hand and said, "No thanks, friend bartender, I'll stick to beer," and in an aside to Vent, counseled, "eat a handful of them peppers with the beer and you'll never notice it tastes like crushed Gila monster."

As the bartender turned to leave, Spencer said, "One moment, friend. A bunch of fellers rode in here about an hour ago. Where are they?"

The bartender looked out toward the street, then asked, "Friends of yours, are they?"

"Let's say we know them," Spencer said.

The bartender did not like this. As was the case with most men in his profession, he never took sides. In a country where all kinds drink at your bar, you couldn't afford to favor one over the other, and you couldn't afford to gossip about any man's business. On the other hand, these three men looked tough and dangerous and fully capable of almost anything. And they were here. The others were not.

"They stopped for a drink and to water their horses and fill canteens, then they went across to the mercantile and bought some grub and rode out," he said.

"Which direction?" Sharp asked.

"West. One of them, the feller in the black chaps, said something about camping a couple of miles from town and waiting."

"Didn't happen to mention who they were waiting for, did they?" Vent asked, and as he put the question, he raised his eyes and looked squarely at the fat man, at the same time picking up a *tortilla* rolled around a mess of beans and holding it in his leather-covered hand.

The man first stared into Vent's cool brown eyes, then dropped his gaze to the hand and stiffened. "No sir, they didn't mention that. I've told you all I know, sir," he said carefully, and he started backing toward the bar.

Looking at him, Vent asked, "You know me?"

The bartender nodded, then swallowed.

"You afraid of me?" Vent asked, and there was genuine curiosity in his voice.

"Well, Mr. Leatherhand, you got a kinda big rep out here," the bartender said. "Folks say you killed some people, that sorta thing."

"Did I ever do you or yours any harm?" Vent persisted.

"No, you sure ain't . . ."

"Then why are you scared of me?"

The bartender shook his head and said, "Can't rightly say, but folks with your kinda reputation, no offense meant, sorta keep other folks edgy . . ."

"Well, relax," Vent said quietly as he turned back to his meal. "I ain't fixing to kill anybody today, leastways no bartenders."

The fat man hurried around the plank and busied himself wiping glasses. He would have a story to tell folks when they came in. How the famous Leatherhand pistol fighter came into his tavern and ate and drank.

At the table Sharp grinned and said, "Never does any good. The meek are supposed to inherit the world, but right now it belongs to the feller with the most guns and the nerve to use them. That feller don't stack up that way."

"You said it," Spencer grunted, stuffing a bean-laden *tortilla* into his mouth and talking around it. "He'll get his reward later, after we're all six feet under in boot hill. Peckerwoods like him will be struttin' around the earth runnin' things. We'll be a memory."

"I'm thinkin' if we don't get the hell outta this town, we're gonna be a memory a damn sight sooner than we planned," Sharp observed and, dropping a coin on the table, went to the door and peered over the batwings into the empty street. Nothing moved but a tired-looking hound wandering down the opposite side of the street, head low and eyes snaking left and right as if he expected to be kicked. Sharp came back and said, "Street's clear."

They went out the back door while the bartender continued to scrub vigorously at his glasses and ignore them. Mounting, they rode down the alley and stopped at the mercantile, tying up to a battered hitchrail whose cross beam was gnawed to splinters by a range full of restless horseflesh left to switch flies while their owners drank in the saloon or bought grub in the store.

Inside it was 20 degrees cooler than on the street, and Sharp removed his hat and brushed his forearm across his forehead, sluicing sweat onto his coat and then looking at it with a fastidious man's disgust.

"What can I do for you, gents?" a man standing behind the counter asked. He was tall, gaunt, and had hands that appeared more suited to the plow than to stacking groceries. Peering at them from beneath a pair of winged white eyebrows under a pate so bald it shone as if it had been rubbed with oil, he smiled an ingratiating smile and leaned back against a row of shelves.

"Need some grub," Spencer said shortly, and the men gathered canned goods, a slab of bacon, some salt, a small sack of flour, and a bag of coffee, and piled it on the counter.

Vent pointed to a stack of ammunition behind the man and said, "Two boxes of forty-fours and two of thirty-eight/forties," and watched as they were placed beside the food.

Sharp had been gazing into a gun case near the door, and now he crooked a finger at the store owner, who came immediately, smelling a sale. Pointing, he asked, "The derringer. How much?"

"That's a forty-four, best they make. Sells for twenty-five dollars, coin," the man said.

Sharp dug up the money and laid it on the counter. When the store man reached for it, Sharp laid a hand over it and said, "I think you should probably throw in a box of forty-fours, don't you?"

Looking into his customers face and not liking what he saw there, the store man nodded and fetched the shells. Picking up the coin and placing it between a husky set of molars, he bit down on it, then flipped it in the air, caught it and stuck it in his pocket.

Vent and Spencer split the cost of the groceries and carried them out to the horses, stuffed them into saddlebags and mounted up.

As they rode north out of town, the blacksmith came to the door, nodded, and waved, saying, "Keep yer powder dry." Vent pulled in and said quietly, "Mr. Morgan, a Torrey never forgets a debt. I'm in yours," and rode on.

"Just so," Sharp said and lit a cigar. He had purchased a double handful in the saloon.

"You get tobacco, Cam?" Vent asked.

"Damn." Spencer turned his horse and rode at a hard trot back into Main Street and dropped off at the store. He came out in a minute or two carrying a small bag and, pushing it into a saddlebag, quickly mounted and rode north again. As he reached the far end of Main Street, he looked back and was in time to see Taper and half a dozen riders turn into the street from the south.

Riding straight ahead, he did not look back again, but continued on until he reached a low place in the desert, then put his horse to a gallop and soon overtook Vent and Sharp. Riding in beside the Missourian, he said conversationally, "Saw a funny thing back there. Mr. Grey

Taper and a whole corral full of tough-looking waddies just rode into town."

Sharp cocked his head to one side and asked just as nonchalantly, "They see you?"

"Nope. I rode right on out. Guess they figured I was some wandering 'poke from one of the ranches around here."

Vent looked over his shoulder and said, "You get the tobacco?"

Spencer stared at Sharp. "Yeah, I got it," Sharp replied and, reaching in his saddlebag, dug out a sack and tossed it to Vent.

Rolling a cigarette, the tall gunfighter thought about Taper behind them and Branda somewhere ahead of them and didn't like it.

"We're kinda in a box here," he said. "Need a way to kick the end out of it."

"Thought of that," Sharp agreed.

Spencer looked over his shoulder but saw nothing and observed, "Seems to me if they closed the pinchers now we'd be caught like bugs on a lamp chimney."

"We could just ride east," Sharp suggested.

Vent shook his head, then asked, "How far you reckon a gunshot carries in this desert country? Three . . . maybe four or five miles?"

Thinking about it Sharp said, "More like five or six."

Looking at Spencer, Vent asked, "Cam?"

"I agree with Sharp."

Looking down the ears of the buckskin, Vent thought about that then suggested, "Let's see if we can find Branda's camp without him seeing us."

"And if he's more than six miles from Two Guns we drop in for a visit," Spencer guessed.

Vent shook his head. "Nope, we first whittle them down. This ain't gonna be no stand-and-fire shoot in the middle of the street and the fastest man wins. We're at war here, and I don't like the odds." Looking at Vent's expression, Sharp decided things were probably going to get just a bit rapid soon.

Spencer said, "Well, it's about damned time. Me, I was gettin' kinda tired of all this here running around, dodging gunslicks and high-binders."

"If Taper had kept the others out, I would say fight him square, but bringing snakes like Hanks and Branda into his camp is another thing. Not only has he outlawed his spread, but he's joined forces with men who sic Comancheros on folks," Vent observed.

Spencer suddenly drew rein and, looking at the ground, said, "Six riders been through here. Not too long ago, either."

Vent had his look, as did Sharp, then they moved on; but caution rode with them as they kept a wary eye on possible ambush spots. It was Spencer who first smelled the smoke and, holding up a hand, motioned for the others to wait for him and rode off in a southwesterly direction. Dismounting, Sharp and Vent squatted on their heels and smoked.

Half an hour passed, and Vent was about ready to ride in after him when Spencer came jogging up and dropped from his horse, reached in Vent's pocket, and lifted his tobacco sack. Rolling a smoke, he said, "They're camped under a big old greasewood about a mile southeast of here. From where I took my look-see, the railroad 'pears to be about five miles due south. I figure they're a good six to seven miles from Two Guns. What now?"

Picking up a stick, Vent handed it to Spencer and said, "Draw me a map of their camp," and watched as Spencer sketched a crude map showing the location of the Branda force's fire beneath the tree, the blanket rolls scattered in a semicircle and the horses tied by a waterhole.

"Looked to me like they wasn't expecting any trouble. They was one man over here." Spencer drew a large rock. "He was sitting up there with a rifle in his lap, but most of the time he kept slapping at bugs and cussing."

"Branda?" Vent asked.

"Him and Hanks were sharing a bottle just to the south of the fire, and that feller Von O'Brien was leaning against the tree watching them and grinning. He's a strange gent, that one is," Spencer said.

Sharp nodded agreement. "You never know in what direction he'll go. He's just as apt to side Branda as he is to turn on him. Unpredictable rattler, and fast as hell with them guns of his."

Vent, looking thoughtful, said, "He'll be the one to watch. I figure Branda's a flash in the powder pan, and Hanks won't buck a stacked deck. He plays the cinches and if the gunsmoke gets too thick, he'll break and run."

Sharp grunted, "I agree. But watch Hanks. He may run a hundred yards then hide and plug you in the back on the way out. He's plumb sneaky."

"Branda will fight because he'll have to," Spencer said. "The way I got this angled out, Branda and Hanks joined forces in spite of what Branda told us. He wants the Jorstad place, and when he messed up at the waterhole, he knew he couldn't try that anymore. Probably figured to hang the killings there at the waterhole on the Injuns. He don't much care about the Jorstad ranch. He ain't no rancher. He's a town man. Once Hanks had the place sewed up, they'd probably draw up some kinda partnership deal."

"Yeah," Sharp said, "and Branda would then probably plug old Hanks in the back and take her all."

Vent grinned. "That's the way I've figured it. They decided to help Taper when I bought into the game and you fellers came in with me. Those boys know they gotta dump us underground before they can lay claim to anything."

"The one thing we don't know here is when this meeting is supposed to come off," Sharp said. "Me, I'd surely dislike having Taper and his boys show up right in the middle of us cutting down Branda's group. That would be damn poor poker."

"Well, then let's cut her loose," Spencer said and went to his horse and stepped into the saddle. Sliding his Winchester free, he jacked a round into the chamber, let it off cock, and, laying it across the saddle swell, said, "Fellers?"

Vent and Sharp mounted up, and the three men rode toward Branda's camp. "Warlike, ain't he?" Sharp observed.

They caught Branda and his men flat-footed. Vent dismounted two hundred feet from the encampment and, walking up a gentle slope, took cover behind a large boulder and had his look. Below him all was peaceful. The fire smouldered beneath a coffeepot, and the men lay sprawled about as if they were on roundup. The lone guard had placed his rifle across his knees and was dozing, head on his chest, his hat slanted to shade his face.

Returning to where Spencer and Sharp sat their horses, Vent said quietly, "Guess one of us had best take that guard out," and Sharp grinned wolfishly, dismounted, conjured up a long, razor-sharp fighting knife, and, holding it by the blade, led his horse off in a long semicircle, coming up to within fifty feet of the sleeping guard. The soft sand muffled the horse's hooves, and now Sharp dropped the reins and, leaving the black tied to the ground, walked casually upright until he was standing directly behind the man.

Vent saw the gambler's arm suddenly whip back and

then drive forward and release the knife, its blade a silver streak in the sun as it darted the short distance and buried itself to the hilt in the man's back.

The sound of the blade tearing flesh was clearly audible where Vent stood. Mounting quickly, he and Spencer gigged their horses and burst over the rise and directly into the camp, guns blazing.

Before the guard had reached the ground from his rock perch, he had three companions on the road to hell and another a split second behind as Vent killed two men scrambling to their feet near Branda and Spencer dropped a third. Both men then fired at Branda and saw him jerk around and pitch into the desert sand on his face, one arm outstretched and clutching at a handful of nothing.

Sharp had leaped onto the rock, and now he poured several pistol shots into the camp, knocking over a man who was attempting to crawl away, dragging a bleeding left leg behind him.

When the shooting started, Von O'Brien had drawn like thunder only to find himself staring into Vent's gun muzzle. Neither man fired in that split second, then the black-clad O'Brien suddenly leaped backward and disappeared from sight down a cutbank. For the next few minutes Vent was too busy to worry about the man, and then the shooting stopped as abruptly as it began and the attackers moved into the encampment, checking their handiwork.

Looking around Sharp asked, "Where the hell's Hanks?"

Spencer had his look, rolling a man over and staring into his dead eyes, then glancing around and shaking his head. "Gone, and so is that gun-slammer, O'Brien."

Vent punched the empties from his pistol, reloaded, and holstered it. "If I don't come back, you fellers head for the border," he said and walked over the lip of the rise, following O'Brien's boot prints in the sand. He found the man waiting a hundred yards from the bullet-plastered camp.

As Vent walked around a large boulder, O'Brien stepped from the cover of some tangled buckbrush fifty feet from him and, standing with one hand on his hip just above his weapon, said, "Mr. Torrey, I have an aversion to gunplay at random; besides, the odds were a little lean. You want me, you're going to have to earn the notch."

Vent had stopped and now he reached up and cocked his hat over his eye with his left hand, keeping his leather-covered right hand near his .44. "You call it, Mr. O'Brien," he said.

"One question?"

"Fire and fall back."

"Why do you wear that thing on your hand?"

Vent grinned. "Old Ute magic. Don't understand it myself, but it gives me twice the normal speed. That's why nobody has ever beaten me."

"I do believe you're pulling my leg," O'Brien said and went for his gun.

Vent shot him twice. The first slug drilled a neat hole in the gunman's left chest, knocking him sideways. As he tried to turn back and get off a shot, Vent planted the second bullet in the center of his chest. The impact slammed O'Brien against a stunted tree and he hung there for just a moment, his eyes trying desperately to focus, then he said, "Damn, you're fast," and collapsed as if all the strings of life had suddenly been cut.

Punching the empties from the .44, Vent reloaded, saluted the dead man with the pistol barrel, and turned and headed back toward the camp, only to discover Spencer lowering his rifle and Sharp lighting a cigar.

Walking up to them, Vent shook his head. "Damn quick, that feller."

Looking at Vent curiously, Spencer asked, "Was that thing you told him about your hand the truth?"

"Reckon it was," Vent opined and walked past them back toward Branda's camp.

When they arrived, they found Branda gone.

Looking toward the horses, Sharp counted them and then said, "Looks like the report of Mr. Branda's death was only a tall tale. He's taken his horse and ridden the hell outta here."

"Who had him under their gun?" Vent asked.

"I thought you nailed him," Spencer said.

"And I thought you took him, Cam," Vent said.

Sharp shook his head. "Now, that feller's one tricky gent. You reckon he and Hanks split the wind together?"

"Nope, unless Branda picked Hanks up later and the two of them headed into the desert on one horse," Vent observed.

"I doubt like hell Branda would take that kinda risk," Sharp argued. "He'd know damn well two fellers on one horse would never make it back to Jerome . . . Unless he planned to make a circle and hightail it back to Two Guns."

They mounted and rode south, Vent in the lead and watching the ground for sign. When they crossed the railroad tracks and had quartered three miles beyond, Vent called off the hunt and they backtracked and repeated the maneuver, riding north this time. There was no sign of either man.

Back at the camp again they took time out for a smoke break as the flies, having discovered the gun-ripped bodies, buzzed over the dead men. Then Vent nodded toward the desert and said, "Owney, you wanta tail Hanks for a ways?"

Sharp nodded, checked his canteen, and mounted. "Where do we meet?"

"Two miles east of Two Guns on the rail line," Vent said and watched Sharp move out. Mounting then, he and Spence rode a crisscross pattern until Vent picked up Branda's horse tracks, then fell in behind them and settled down to the steady gait of the pursuer.

Hanks stood staring at the Indian as the Apache raised his rifle and sighted it on his head. "Unbuckle the gunbelt," the Indian ordered, and when Hanks hesitated, snapped, "do it or die."

Cursing, Hanks let his weapon fall and, when the Indian gestured, stepped away from the gunbelt and waited. He had walked for two hours, then, knowing one of Vent's friends would be on his tail, began hiding his tracks. At one point he broke off a bush and switched out his back trail for half a mile until he became so dizzy from the lack of water and the heat he was forced to quit. A bit later he came upon a stretch of windswept rock and followed it for at least three miles. It was while working his way through a pile of blasted boulders scattered over a field fifty acres wide that he caught a glimpse of a rider following him and took refuge behind a boulder, pistol in hand. The rider apparently gave up the pursuit before he reached Hanks's ambush and turned back. Knowing he must do the same soon or die of thirst, the fugitive began a long swing north and east in an attempt to reach Two Guns again.

He was at the apex of that circle and about to swing south when the Indian rode from behind a rock and pointed the rifle at him.

The Apache Kid was elated. He had had a rough time since the woman knocked him unconscious and left him tied naked for the vultures to feed on. It had been a simple matter for him to slip the ropes and leave, and because he was a child of the desert, he survived simply until he stumbled onto a fight between a group of riders and two white men. While they shot at each other, the Kid killed the horse handler and mounted one of the horses, then, hearing voices, dropped behind a rock and forted up, waiting to kill whoever appeared around the bend of the canyon.

When a tall man wearing shotgun chaps and a low-tied pistol appeared, sided by a man dressed all in black who had apparently been wounded in the fight up the canyon, the Kid leveled his rifle, took aim, and prepared to pick them off. Then it happened. The man in black went into action, opening fire on him from a pistol so swiftly drawn that it caught the Apache completely by surprise. Then the second man was afoot and using his horse for cover, and the Kid knew these were not just cowboys but experienced fighting men. He ran, mounted the stolen horse, still without a stitch on, and galloped away.

Now he had a white man under his rifle. It was time to even the score and change his luck back to where it had been before he captured that accursed girl and allowed her to escape.

"Walk that way," the Kid said, pointing his rifle toward a grove of gnarled trees growing in among the boulders.

As the white man trudged toward the trees, the Apache Kid slid from his horse and followed on foot. When they reached the trees, he made the man move between two of them and, using pieces of rawhide, tied his wrists and ankles so that he was spread-eagled. Standing back, he said, "White man, when I was on the reservation and made to attend your white man's school, they taught me about your god and how he died when his enemies nailed his hands and feet to a cross. Your people told me this is a very noble and brave way to die and that when your god died that way, he came back and talked to them. Our gods do not come back as humans. They come back as the wolf, the coyote, the bear and the wind and the thunder. They talk to us, but not in our language."

Bending then, the Kid removed a large knife from his right legging and, testing the edge with his thumb, smiled at the white man.

"They also told me in that white man's school that your god was tortured and because of that he was blessed," the Kid said. Stepping up to the cringing, bug-eyed white man, he told him, "Now I am going to do you a great service. I am going to help you become blessed," and with a flick of the wrist, the Kid slit the man's shirt from shoulder to waist then tore it away, baring his heaving chest. Next he cut away his pants and his boots, finally ripping off the long johns all white men seemed to favor.

Stepping away, the Kid went to his horse and removed a canteen, drank deep of its contents while watching the white man's face, then tied the horse to a mesquite bush in case the white man's shrieks of agony frightened the animal. The Kid did not want to have to take the time to steal another horse.

As the Kid approached him the white man said huskily, "Look, Injun, you give me a break and I'll show you where they's over a hundred head of prime beef just for the taking. Hell, I'll even help you."

The Kid stared at him with unblinking eyes, then said, "And where are these cows you speak of?"

"They're on my ranch over west of here. You help me and I'll give 'em to you."

The Kid spit at the man's feet and grinned. "Al

Siebert, the man who taught me many things, would say of this offer that it is just another white man's trick and will only lead to a hole in the head and another in the ground."

"You . . . you worked for Siebert?" the white man stammered.

"I was his scout," the Kid said, then pounded his chest with his fist and said proudly, "I am the Apache Kid."

The white man's face seemed to almost fall in on itself, and the Kid, watching him, glorified in his obvious fear as he raised the knife and made his first cut, then stepped back and listened to his victim's horrified scream. The sound was music to his ears.

The Kid later admitted the white man's endurance had been surprising. He had managed to live through six hours of agony under the Kid's knife before the blessed relief of death came to release him from the torture. With a last hideous shriek of pain, the white man's body had jerked, twitched uncontrollably, and then his chin dropped onto his chest and his blood-drenched body hung limp and dead.

The Kid stepped forward and lifted his victim's chin and stared into the half-closed eyes and saw only blankness there. Grunting, he suddenly plunged the blade deep in the white man's chest, then dragged it downward, emptying the body cavity onto the desert sands. Leaning down, he picked up the torn long-handles and wiped the bloody blade clean, then, tossing them to one side, walked to his horse, mounted, and rode west. As he reached the top of a small sand dune, he looked back and watched as the desert wind tossed up a thin film of dust then pushed the corpse of the white man in a quarter turn and, subsiding, allowed it to swing gently back to its former position.

Chapter VIII

Vent sat his horse on a low rise to the east of Dry Springs and watched the thin line of riders moving in off the desert and down the town's Main Street. A fine powdering of trail dust drifted in behind them, then was snatched away by the wind and pushed south. The same wind twitched the brim of Vent's Stetson and ruffled the handkerchief at his throat. He sat alone on the buckskin and considered a number of things he could do now, but hesitated over each piece of action. There were nine riders down there dismounting in front of the Red Horse Saloon, and Vent knew they had to be the worst of the fifty Taper had started with. He figured the others, most of them common range riders and ranch hands, had drifted away, not wanting their names linked with an outlaw spread. Even from where he sat the line-back buckskin, he could pick out the huge shape of Grey Taper and the slighter form of Cole Butram. The rest of the mongrel pack was the leavings and scrapings found on almost any ranch in that time in history. They were the opportunists, the reckless and the owlhoot, the night rider who had taken a job for a season, or until he found a chance to ride off with another man's cows or horses, the gunslammers, such as Butram and Shorty Hodge, or the calloused old pro Vance Caudell, who hung on because he had nowhere else to go.

These were the men left to Grey Taper, and they were the worst kind. Vent figured that once they killed him, they would take the outlaw trail. Many gangs began from such a start. A rancher committed a rash act and went on the dodge. Some of his men went with him. There was the other possibility: Taper, having killed Vent, would rebuild his ranch headquarters and be stronger than ever, growing on Vent's reputation. If that happened, he would eventually begin to spread out until his holdings would require a veritable army to police. The more men he hired, the more power he would yield. Vent knew there were other outfits like that; some were legitimate, such as the King Ranch down in Texas, a spread so huge that they said a man could ride from the Canadian River to old Mexico and camp on King Ranch property every night. Such outfits often experienced alarming stock losses, the kind of losses that would break a smaller ranch, but only forced the big owner to hire an army of hardcase gunslammers to ride the borders and guard against thievery. Sometimes these men were over-eager in the pursuit of outlaws and stretched the wrong neck by accident. Such haste precluded apology, Vent knew, and because this did occur, many cowboys steered a wide path around the big outfits, usually going to the nearest town, if seeking work.

As Vent watched, Taper's men disappeared inside the saloon, but the big man paused on the front porch and, standing beneath the porch roof, shaded his eyes and gazed down street. Vent looked that way and saw the stagecoach coming and just to the east of it the train, its funnel-shaped bell-stack spouting smoke. Its whistle came to where Vent sat the buckskin, and its lonesome wail reminded him suddenly of the day when he stood on the platform of a train station in the mountains of Colorado and looked over a shotgun barrel at Hitch Hawks, the last of the Torreys' traditional enemies. Vent had let him live, but now wondered if he had it to do over again he would follow the same path. Probably, he thought, and realized that was what separated him from men like Owney Sharp, who had reached a point of no return.

He had split up with Sharp and Spencer near Two Guns, leaving them to try and track Branda down. Now, as he watched Taper, the big man tossed a burned-out cigar into the dust of the street and walked toward the stage, his hat pulled low to shade his eyes, his heavy, rawhide batwing chaps flapping around his legs. Watching him, Vent wondered what made a man into a Grey Taper. What drive pushed a man who already had more than his share to attempt to acquire even more, riding roughshod over all in his way, killing folks and taking what he pleased.

"Just plain ornery," Vent murmured, and then the stage pulled to a stop in front of the Wells Fargo office in a billow of dust amid the sounds of the whip shouting curses at his team. Several people stepped from the stage and moved out of the dust and up on the sidewalk. Vent could imagine the driver warning those who were traveling through that he would be moving out in twenty minutes and the man who wasn't there was the man who got left.

As Vent watched, a stocky man in a worn business suit and cavalry hat met Taper in front of the stage station and shook hands, then the big rancher slapped him on the back, and the two men walked back down the street and pushed through the batwings into the Red Horse Saloon.

"Now, I wonder who that jasper is?" Vent asked himself, and at the sound of his voice his horse pricked up its ears and then dropped its head and lazily pulled at the dry buffalo grass that grew around the bottoms of the sagebrush he stood in.

Vent watched the saloon for another ten minutes, then turned his horse away and rode north.

Inside the Red Horse, Taper's men were lined up along the bar, full glasses before them, joking and kidding each other when their boss came through the batwings, followed by a quiet-faced man wearing a cavalry hat and dusty business suit. A blond mustache framed his mouth. At first glance he could have been mistaken for a down-at-the-heels grubline rider, but anyone who was sober and had the time to look into the man's eyes and watch his hands as they rested lightly near the smooth bone handles of a pair of Colt Peacemakers would know different.

"Boys, want you to meet a friend of mine," Taper called, and his men immediately stopped talking and turned as one man. Cole Butram, in the middle of a joke, cut it off and had his look, made his assessment of the stranger, and waited. Tuck Willoby cleaned his fingernails on his Bowie and looked at the floor. Vance Caudell, whose only weakness was saloon women, gently lifted the little blond dance hall girl from his lap and, patting her on the rear, whispered something that brought a smile to her face. She stood leaning on his shoulder and stared curiously at the stranger.

"This here's Henry Brown, the marshal of Caldwell, Kansas," Taper said, and nodding to the bartender, said, "Harp, set us up a bottle."

There were blank faces around the room until Cole Butram, who had spent some time down in Lincoln County, New Mexico, in 1878, looked hard at the man, then, as Taper led him to a table, walked over and sat opposite Caudell and said, "That feller was with Bill

Bonney down in Lincoln County during the stockman's war."

"So he's a marshal now, huh?" Caudell mused.

"Yep, and they say he's a damn fast man with a gun," Butram grunted. "You reckon Taper figures to sic that gent onto Leatherhand?"

Then Taper lifted a lazy hand and motioned, and Butram went to his table and sat down and endured Brown's scrutiny as Taper said, "Mr. Brown here, he's got kind of a unique ability. He can draw and fire a sidearm about as fast as anybody around. I told him if he wanted to get in some real live practice, I would pay him five thousand dollars to shoot several holes in them two pards of Leatherhand's."

"You figure you can beat Sharp, Mr. Brown?" Butram asked, watching Brown's eyes.

They did not change expression as he said in a dull monotone, "I'll kill him . . . either through the front or the back."

"They say he's got eyes in the back of his head," Butram grinned.

"Every man's time comes and this is Sharp's," Taper said and poured Brown another drink.

Watching the cold-eyed blond gunfighter, Butram began recalling some of the things he had heard about this man. In Texas and New Mexico, Brown was well known for his vicious nature. He was a known horse thief, making a specialty out of lifting horses from the Pecos country and running them into the Panhandle, where he sold them off. Well known along the southern cattle trails, nobody could figure out how he managed to land the job in Caldwell, although Butram had heard the gunfighter served somewhere in Texas for a short while as a deputy sheriff.

Taper lifted his glass and said, "To a tight cinch and a

full cartridge belt. Been a long time, Henry. How they treating you up there in Caldwell?"

"Just got married," Brown said shortly.

"Hell, that's worth a celebration." He handed Brown a cigar and nipped the end off a second one, sticking it unlit in the corner of his mouth. Brown slid his in his vest pocket, then rose and said, "I'll go down to the stage station and pick up my gear and get settled in."

When he started to move around the table, Taper held up a restraining hand and, nodding at Butram, said, "Cole, get one of the boys to go down and pick up Henry's stuff, will you?"

Butram nodded and went to the bar, tolled off a man, and sent him away, then stayed there, quietly sipping the whiskey Harp Sinclair had placed in front of him. He did not like Taper bringing in this hired gun. It would serve the bastard right if Sharp punched his ticket, Butram thought as Caudell slid in beside him and nodded at Sinclair to set him up.

"Don't like our Mr. Brown, huh?" he asked.

"Nope, but I don't reckon I'm gonna tell him that," Butram said.

"That good, is he?"

"Better than that," Butram nodded. "He just might shove Sharp off."

A small puncher with his hat on the back of a cueball-smooth head grunted and said, "I seen this here Brown slap leather down in Lincoln County once. He's fast as billy-be-damned but I also seen Sharp plug a gunsel in Tombstone one time when the feller had him shaded by at least three seconds. Sharp killed him."

"Then you figure Brown ain't no match for Sharp?" Butram asked.

"I'll bet a month's pay on it," the bald cowboy said.

"You're on, Pete," Butram said, and Caudell, looking

over at Brown, thought about it for a minute and said, "I'll take Brown, but I want three-to-one odds."

"Two to one," Pete promptly shot back.

"Two to one it is," Caudell agreed.

The Taper rider came in with Brown's gear and, walking over to the table, asked, "You staying at the ranch, Mr. Brown, or in town?"

"Beds any good here?" the marshal asked.

"They ain't got no bedbugs in 'em, leastways they didn't the last time I stayed here, but then, I was too busy to pay much attention." Taper grinned.

Glancing at one of the saloon girls standing near the stairway, Brown said, "If she comes in the bargain, I'll hang around."

Taper, somewhat taken aback since Brown had just announced he was recently married, cleared his throat. "I guess that can be worked out. Cole, come here," he called, and watched as the foreman left the bar and walked over, his spurs rattling on the planks.

"See that girl"—and Taper pointed her out—"I believe her name's Ann or Anna or something like that. Tell her she's to keep Mr. Brown company while he's here . . ."

Butram stared at Taper, then looked at Brown, whose eyes were faintly amused, and said, "Mr. Taper, I'm a stockman. I ain't no pimp. If this feller wants a woman, then he's gonna have to do his own gettin'."

Taper stared at Butram for a long minute while Brown, eyes still amused, let his hand fall toward his gun butt. Glancing at him, Butram said quietly, "Mr. Taper, this here gent's got a fearsome rep and I surely don't hanker to swap pills with him. If he pulls on me I'm gonna ignore him and kill you where you set, and you know damn well that even if he gets lead into me, I'm gonna get off at least one shot. At this range, I can't miss."

Taper stared at his foreman, then glancing at Brown,

said, "I didn't ask you here to plug my foreman, Henry. Let it go. I'll talk to Harp. Hell, it's his girl and he's the feller who profits."

Brown moved his hand back onto the tabletop and smiled at Butram. "You got you one slick foreman here, Grey. This gent ain't no fool, nor does he lack nerve. Best keep him around," he said, and he rose and went to the girl at the end of the bar. He whispered something to her, and she followed him upstairs as he led the way, bag in hand.

Taper watched Butram move to the bar. He did not resent his foreman's actions. In fact, if Butram had allowed himself to be used in that way, Taper would have seriously considered replacing him with one of the other men.

Boots Thomas had his feet up on his big old hardwood desk when Spencer and Sharp came through the office doorway. Leaning far back in his swivel chair, he stared at them between his polished boot toes, then asked nobody in particular, "What I'd like to know is how the hell Owney Sharp can ride a hundred miles through the dust and sand of the Painted Desert or some other godforsaken place and arrive at the end of his journey looking as if he just stepped from the pages of a men's clothing catalogue."

Grinning, Owney sat down in a chair near the back wall and carefully began peeling the wrapping from a cigar.

"He always has a change of clothes with him," Spencer explained.

"Hell, I figured he toted along a Chinese laundryman wherever he went," Thomas said.

"You got anything to cut a man's whistle, or we gonna have to venture out to some saloon and take a chance on getting all shot fulla holes by some of Branda's men?" Sharp asked.

Reaching into a desk drawer, Thomas came up with a bottle of whiskey and handed it around. Each man had his drink. Thomas then placed it in the center of his desk between his knees and said, "Hep yourself, boys, till she's gone."

The door opened and Del Woods came in and hung his hat on a peg near the door. Lifting a coffeepot off the old iron stove sitting near the back of the office, he shook it, then turned and went to the desk and, picking up the bottle, said, "Ain't it hell when a man's forced to drink whiskey because the coffee's done gone?" and took a huge swallow.

Nodding at him, Thomas said solemnly, "When I first met Del and hired him as my deputy, I couldn't figure out how come he was always getting drunk. He never took more than a mouthful. Then I measured his mouth and it held a quart."

Soft chuckles met this sally, then Thomas lowered his feet to the floor, being careful not to spill the bottle. "What brings you cold-eyed gunnies into my territory?" he asked casually.

"Had a little set-to with Hazen Branda over near Two Guns. His boys is all dead . . . including O'Brien . . ." Sharp said.

Woods and Thomas stared at them. "Von O'Brien's dead?" Thomas asked and then, shaking his head, said, "Who got him?"

"Vent. They shot her out fair and square," Spencer told him. "Me and Owney, we watched it. I tell ya, Boots, we never saw Vent draw that damn forty-four. He just sorta magicked it up out of his holster. Caught O'Brien flat-flooted."

"We tailed Branda back here after we ran out a trail on Butch Hanks," Sharp said.

"Yeah, you can scratch him too. There's one gent who'll never again turn loose the Comancheros on some innocent rancher," Sharp noted.

"He sicked them varmits on Jorstad?" Thomas asked.

"Yep, sure as hell did, but he's keeping that bunch that hit Wag's place company," Spencer said. "They're all dead."

"Who got Hanks?" Woods asked.

"We didn't," Sharp said. "He ran. We found him out in the desert tied between a coupla trees. He was dead as a nit. Looked like somebody had spent a year chopping and cutting at him with a double-bitted axe. They left him with his guts dragging the ground."

"Jesus!" Woods said reverently.

"So, Branda came home to roost?" Thomas asked.

"Yeah. Reckon he's down at the Devil's Rondeevoo," Sharp said. Then he rose, looked at Spencer, and asked, "Shall we go fetch him?"

Thomas went to a rack and, reaching up, took down a double-barreled shotgun and broke it, checking the loads. Satisfied it was ready, he went to his desk and stuffed his pockets with more shells from a desk drawer.

"This ain't your fight," Sharp declared.

"My town. My fight," Thomas said. "Del, you take a rifle and go on down to the other end of the street and keep it under your gun. Me and the boys here will just toddle on down and see if we can't persuade Mr. Branda that it's time for him to come pay the fiddler." Shotgun under his arm, Thomas led the way.

As they passed through the door, Sharp looked down at the murderous weapon and saw it was a sawed-off model commonly referred to as a "Greener," manufactured in the 1800s by a man called Green. A Greener gave the man carrying one a decided firepower edge over his opponent.

As the three men walked abreast along the street, loafing cowhands stared, then dodged into doorways. Their women quickly ducked inside stores and peeked from windows. Several men who had left horses along the street quickly exited buildings, untied their animals and led them into alleys or down street and onto one of the cross streets. No one spoke to the three grim men as they reached the Devil's Rondeevoo and turned through the batwings.

As they entered the big barroom, several patrons looked up, gulped their whiskey with a quick flip of the wrist, and vanished out the back door. The Negro fiddler sawed his instrument off abruptly, picked up his coin can, and slipped through the front door as several bar girls hurried up a staircase near the back of the room.

Branda stood at the bar, clothes covered with dust and his shirt sticking to his body with the sweat of his recent ride from Two Guns, his green eyes glittering in the bar light like broken shards of glass.

He wore a pair of crossed gunbelts and stood with thumbs hooked into them near the butts of two Colts. As he stared at the trio, sweat dripped from his handlebar mustache and splattered on the front of his vest, kicking up tiny bomb bursts of dust and leaving spots of wetness resembling bullet holes.

Thomas let his eyes flick around the room, first spotting the shotgunner on the balcony, who was slowly swiveling his weapon in an attempt to bring it to bear on the men by the door without being spotted. A second man leaned against the end of the bar with his right hand hidden in front of him. Thomas guessed he probably held a pistol under his coat ready for instant use. The bartender had both hands beneath the plank and was watching Thomas narrowly.

"Mr. Branda, you are under arrest," Thomas said.

"Huh?" Branda grunted.

"Arrest . . . You know. That's when I put the handcuffs on you and take you off to the calaboose," Thomas explained patiently.

Branda grinned. "Boots, you always was a card."

Suddenly the room was filled with an eerie crooning sound that jerked all eyes toward the back.

"What the hell was that?" Branda asked in awe.

When the shot came nobody was prepared for it. One moment Branda was staring at the back door and the next parts of his skull were exploding backward toward the mirror. At the same instant Thomas tilted his shotgun and fired the left hand barrel into the man on the balcony, who screamed in high, wild agony, bounded back against the wall and then pitched forward to somersault over the rail and drop into the middle of a card table near the end of the bar.

Sharp drew and killed the man at the end of the plank just as he spun and lifted his hideout gun. The gambler's bullet drilled a neat hole in the center of the man's left pocket and he jerked sideways, grunted sharply, and seemed to fold in on himself as he collapsed on top of a spitoon, spilling it.

Spencer, who had been watching a narrow door behind the bartender, first shot that worthy through the throat then put a second round into the door, which was promptly jerked wide as a man with a rifle toppled backward, still clinging to the doorknob.

The action had been so fast, Branda's body was just hitting the floor as the final shot was fired.

Staring around, Thomas asked wonderingly, "Now,

who in the hell—" and was interrupted by another terrible moaning cry.

Looking at the other men, he strode to the hall doorway and, gun in hand, jerked it open. A woman stood there clutching a rifle, and as Thomas pulled the door back, she dropped it on the floor and sagged into his arms. Carefully, he carried her inside and seated her in a chair. Looking up as Woods burst through the door, rifle at the ready, he said, "Go fetch Doc, quick," and watched Woods skid to a stop, stare wildly around at the blasted bodies littering the floor, and then reverse himself and dodge back outside again.

"Any of you fellers know this woman?" Thomas asked.

"I know her," a voice said from the hallway, and Lud McKiver suddenly found himself looking down the barrels of three guns. Holding up his hands palms out, he came into the room and, kneeling before the woman, said softly, "It's all right, Bonnie May. It's all over now. It's gonna be all right."

McKiver rose and led Thomas down the room, explaining, "That's Bonnie May Doolin, Jimmie Doolin's maw. She's been kinda poorly since the boy got kilt up at our waterhole. I guess she nailed Branda because he was the man who led the raid on us."

As the two men stood talking, a small, bustling man hurried through the door and set a black bag on the table near the woman and stared around. "Looks to me like you done sent all these here fellers off to hell, Boots. What you need me for?"

Thomas nodded at the woman. "She's acting kinda funny, Doc. Reckon maybe you better look her over."

The doctor knelt and tilted the woman's head back and peered at her eyes, then looked around at Thomas and ordered, "Get her up to my office. I need to check her with some of my instruments."

Thomas turned to Woods, who had entered with the doctor, and said, "Del, you give Doc a hand while I get the undertaker over here to clean up this mess."

An hour later the bodies had been moved to a funeral parlor, and Thomas had sacked up all the money he could find in the place and sent it over to the bank to be deposited, with orders to bring back a deposit slip. Then he locked up the Devil's Rondeevoo and pocketed the key. Looking at Spencer and Sharp, he said, "Seems to me wherever you fellers and that sidekick of yours, Vent Torrey, go somebody gets plugged. You fellers won't take it unkindly if I suggest that you kinda ride on outta my jurisdiction, will you?"

"Happy to, Marshal, just as soon as we pick up Vent's Appy. He sure enough misses that horse," Sharp said.

A half an hour later the two men were again riding east. They had stopped long enough to pick up grub and the Appaloosa and fill their water jugs and now they were anxious to connect with Vent.

Sharp cleared his throat. "Funny thing," he said. "Branda going out that way . . ."

Spencer shrugged and said, "Odd kinda justice, I call it."

It was three o'clock in the morning, and Dry Springs had long since rolled up its sidewalks as Vent walked along an alley off the main street until he reached the back of the Jinglebob Cafe. Pausing long enough to make a careful examination of the buildings on both sides of the cafe, and satisfied no one was staked out in one of their doorways or behind a darkened window, he tapped lightly on the back door and waited.

"Who's there?" someone called, and Vent heard the distinct snick of a hammer being drawn back.

"Vent," the Missourian said quietly, and when the

door opened he slid sideways into a dark hallway and followed the hulking shape of the cafe owner back to his bedroom. A lamp glowed dully on a bedstand, and the blankets were thrown back, indicating Shipley had been sleeping. Leaning the rifle in a corner near the head of the bed, the cafe owner sat on its edge and grinned.

"This here town's crawling with Taper's men," he said.

"I seen 'em. Where they staying?"

"Most of them are over in the rooms above the Red Horse, but a couple of those fellers went down and holed up at the livery."

Vent nodded. "Need a bite to eat. I could chew the rear out of a southbound skunk and never notice the smell."

Shipley rose and, pants sagging over his bare feet, led Vent to the kitchen and quickly put together two roast beef sandwiches. Poking up the fire, he pushed the pot on to heat up again.

"Trouble came to town on the stage," Shipley said as he set the sandwiches in front of Vent and watched him dig in.

"Trouble? That feller in the cavalry hat, he the trouble?"

Shipley nodded and poured them both a cup of coffee. "That's Henry Brown from up Caldwell way. Gunfighter, to hear Taper tell it."

"Heard of him," Vent said. "Thought he was marshaling."

"He is. Marshal of Caldwell."

Vent drank deep from the coffee cup, washing down a huge bite of roast beef, and looked up at Shipley. "Then what's he doing around here?"

"No friend of Taper's, even though Taper claims different. Seems kinda funny, now don't it? Here's this pistol fighter, who once rode with the Kid down in New

Mexico, and he comes sashaying into Dry Springs loaded for bear. Gonna stomp some of Grey Taper's snakes, he is."

Vent thought on that as Shipley sliced him a huge slab of apple pie and decorated its crown with a gob of butter. "So he hired a fighter, huh?"

"Not for you, he didn't," Shipley said. "Those boys of his are betting three to one Brown ices Owney Sharp. Harp heard 'em talking up in Brown's room after he closed and they were making a deal for Brown to put a bullet into both Spencer and Sharp. Sort of strip away your help . . ."

"An' me?" Vent asked, chewing at the pie, which was among the best he had ever eaten. "Good pie," he added, and Shipley smiled broadly and brought him another slice.

"Once Cam and Owney are out of the way, Taper figures you'll be easy. He still plans to hang you to that big oak in his front yard."

"I oughta go cut it down," Vent said and moved to the back door. Carefully opening it a crack he had his look up the alley and then stepped outside and shook Shipley's hand. "I'll be out at May's old place. If Cam and Owney happen to miss me and come here, tell them where I'm at. Warn 'em about Brown. Owney probably knows him, but in case he don't, tell him I said the man's almost as fast as I am and probably faster than Luke Short."

"Luke Short?" Shipley went back inside the cafe shaking his head.

Vent had once seen Short in a gunfight in Wichita, Kansas, when Vent was just a boy. Then he had marveled at the man's snakelike speed, but looking back on it now he realized Short's ace was his rock-steady nerve. No matter what happened, he never became rattled. Thinking about that, Vent realized most of the good men in his profession were of the same caliber, slow and pedantic. Some were overweight and one or two actually very slow. The thing they did have was the nerve to stand fast under fire and take their time lining up their shots.

Men like Hickok were another matter, Vent knew. Hickok was a marvelous gun handler, who often shot by instinct. He seldom if ever missed and never when it counted. Vent knew he fell into that same category. He possessed that uncanny ability not only to draw and fire a pistol in a split second, but also the ability to hit what he aimed at and the further ability to stand under fire.

Now, as he jogged the line-back buckskin along the trail north, he kept his eyes ever roaming from bush to rock to stunted piñon, always expecting an ambush, a bushwacker, or some other threat. The one thing men like Vent could not protect themselves against was the man who laid in wait with a rifle and fired from cover. The only shading in the pistol fighter's favor was the sure and certain knowledge in the back of the bushwacker's mind that if he missed, he would die very suddenly and no one would mourn his passing. In fact, he would probably be left for the buzzards, with no one coming forward to provide him with a Christian burial.

Before riding to the spring at May's old cabin, Vent carefully circled the area. Seeing no one, he rode down boldly and stepped off his horse in a small grove of trees near the spring; then he loosened the cinch and dropped the reins, letting the horse feed on the rich, spring-fed grasses that grew knee high here.

Unrolling his bedding, he built a small fire in a niche in the rocks and, once it was burning well, filled his battered coffeepot and dumped in a handful of grounds. Pushing it into the edge of the coals, he settled back on his bedroll, carefully rolled a cigarette and, tucking it into the corner of his mouth, reached with his left hand to lift out a burning stick. Just as he touched it to his cigarette, a voice said coldly, "Feller could get shot doing that."

Vent finished lighting his cigarette, tossed the burning stick back on the blaze, and said mildly, "'Lo, Henry. Dig out your cup. Coffee's about ready," and let the hammer back down on the .44.

Brown slid into the campsite and squatted across the fire from Vent, placed a battered tin cup on the ground, and reached for a lighted stick to fire up a cigar. "Careful feller," he said, adding, "Taper don't seem to care much for you." He did not smile.

"I put away his son. Guess that sorta shoved him onto the warpath," Vent said.

"From what I hear Bert Taper wasn't worth the powder and lead to blow him to perdition."

"He wasn't," Vent agreed. "Taper knew that. He read the boy's pedigree a long time ago. Has something to do with his dead wife. A promise to take care of Bert. Felt an obligation, I reckon."

"Says he's gonna hang you," Brown said and held out his cup while Vent filled it with steaming coffee.

"So he says," Vent agreed.

"You kinda whittled away some of his resolve," Brown grunted, sipping the hot fluid and making a face.

"You know Owney Sharp?" Vent asked.

"Yeah. Met him in Nogales once. Honest gambler. Best man with a gun I ever saw . . . can you beat him?"

"Yes," Vent said and sipped his coffee.

"Umm . . ."

"You a friend of Taper's?" Vent asked, watching Brown's face.

"No. Just got hitched. Need the money. Need it real bad. Damn marshaling job don't pay nothing."

"Ain't that the way?" Vent agreed. "Town folks can't handle the hard element that comes into their bailiwick so they hire somebody like me or you to risk our necks every day and pay us beans."

Brown looked at Vent and observed, "You've done your share of marshaling."

"So I have," Vent agreed.

"What you figure to come out of this with, that is, if old Taper don't manage to get that noose around your neck?"

"Nothing," Vent said. "It's a free ride. This time I'm working for me. Means I can't just ride out. Was somebody else, I'd figure the odds on this one and hit the dusty. Now it's my backside Taper wants. Can't run."

"No, I understand that . . . If I take a hand with Spencer and Owney, where will you be?"

Vent looked up. "I reckon I'd have to kill you, Henry."

Brown nodded. "I was afraid of that. Well, I never was one to nibble off more than I could chew. Reckon I'll just amble back up north and take care of Caldwell."

"Taper pay you?"

"Why, as a matter of fact, he did," Brown said, and now there was just the hint of a smile in his eyes as he rose and tossed the remainder of his coffee to one side. "It seems he wanted me in this so bad he paid in advance. Now, me, I hate to backtrack over old ground. Reckon I'll just keep going. I rented this here horse at the stable and I reckon he'll get me home."

Brown went to the horse and mounted, then rode back and sat looking down at Vent. "Take care, Leatherhand," he said and left as quietly as he had come.

Carefully, Vent banked his small fire, then, suddenly so tired he could hardly hold up his hand, he spread his blankets near the big rock he had used as shelter from the evening wind. After he had checked the buckskin and restaked him in a fresh patch of grass, after allowing him to drink from the small pool at the base of the spring, he returned to his bedroll.

Placing his pistol near his right hand, he dozed fitfully for a long time, snapping awake at every little sound that disrupted the night's stillness. Finally, too exhausted to stay awake any longer and feeling fairly safe here in a place that Taper had already visited and left, he dropped off into a deep sleep.

Vent rose just as the sun was pushing its dull orb over the eastern edge of the earth. He filled his coffeepot and placed it in the coals of his stoked up fire.

"You'll never drink that coffee," Taper said, and Vent turned to face the big rancher, who stood not thirty feet away, holding a sawed-off shotgun squarely aligned with his chest.

As Vent played with the notion of trying to outdraw Taper's trigger finger, Cole Butram stepped from behind a rock, and, lifting his six-shooter, pointed it casually in Vent's direction. "You might get him," he observed, "but they ain't no way in God's name you'll take me out too. They just ain't enough time."

"Looks like your time has run its string, Mr. Leatherhand," Vance Caudell observed as he came around a clump of bushes, .45 in hand.

Then the clearing was full of Taper riders, and Vent relaxed and thought bitterly, somebody talked. He could only hope Sharp and Spencer got away.

"Bring his horse," Taper ordered, and looking at him, Vent saw the triumph in his eyes and on his blunt features.

"Get his gun," Taper barked and added, "Watch this peckerwood. He's full of all kinds of snake tricks, like the one he used to kill my son."

Vent stared at him. "Your son couldn't outdraw my six-year-old niece," he said scornfully, and looking straight into the rancher's eyes, added, "an' neither can you."

Taper didn't like it, but he held his temper. "I'd face you, Mr. Leatherhand, and in a fair fight with winner taking all, but I swore to hang you to the oak tree in my front yard and, by the lord Harry, that's what I'm gonna do."

"Fine. Let's you and me shoot her out, then your boys can hang me. That way I'll have company on the road to hell," and Vent smiled wickedly.

Caudell, his eyes holding a faint ribbon of amusement, led Vent's horse up and watched him mount, noting, "Too bad you ain't ridin' that there Appaloosa. Feller oughta go out on his own horse."

Staring at him, Vent asked, "How the hell would you know?"

Caudell turned his back on Vent and, without answering, led the buckskin out front and handed the reins to Taper, who turned and said, "Now for the parade through town. Gotta show these folks nobody can buffalo Grey Taper."

"All it'll show them is Grey Taper has the money to pay a bunch of lead-slingers. It sure as hell won't wipe away that yeller streak down your spine, Mr. Taper."

Suddenly savagely angry, Taper whipped the reins around and slashed Vent across the face with them, raising a vicious welt. "Shut yer damn mouth," he growled.

"Brave as hell, beating up a helpless man," Vent said and dove straight into Taper, knocking him off his horse and onto the ground. When Taper managed his feet, Vent sledge-hammered a sizzling right to his face and felt the satisfying crunch of bone collapsing. Taper staggered back, blood squirting from his broken nose, then, eyes filled with madness, bore into Vent's fists, taking half a dozen smashing blows to his chest just over his heart and a whistling punch that ripped his right ear. Then Taper managed to land a blow and the force of it picked Vent up and hurled him onto his back beneath Butram's horse's hooves. A hoof grazed Vent's head as he scrambled to get clear, then he was up and meeting Taper's rushing power, and again he took the dirt as the big rancher slugged a fist like a maul into the side of his head, turning his ear into blood and pulp.

Vent circled the rancher, head tucked into his shoulder, waiting for an opening as the big man stood with arms hanging at his sides and watched his quarry with savage hate.

"I'm . . . gonna . . . kill you . . . with my bare . . . hands . . . you bastard," he grated.

Vent laughed deep in his throat and taunted, "You do that, big man, and you'll miss the hanging," and hurled a roundhouse that split Taper's lip wide open.

Taper rushed forward like a bull on larkspur poison and drove his head into Vent's stomach, knocking the wind from the smaller man and dumping him in the sand. Rolling away just in time to avoid a slashing boot, Vent came to his knees, then rose to his feet and turned to discover his opponent standing looking at him over the twin bores of his shotgun.

Jerking both hammers back with trembling hands, he choked out, "Now you're dead, gunfighter," and with suddenly fatalistic acceptance, Vent relaxed and waited for the tearing impact of the double-ought buck.

"You pull that trigger and I'll shoot you, Mr. Taper." Vance Caudell stood just to the left of the rancher with his .45 aimed at the back of Taper's head.

Whirling on Caudell, Taper asked in wonder, "What the hell's got into you now?"

"Hang the man and I'll help rig the noose," Caudell

said, adding, "although it's a miserable way for a man like this here feller to die. But I ain't gonna stand by and watch you gut-shoot him because he was whipping you in a fair fight. He's dead game and he deserves more . . ."

Glancing at Butram, Taper said softly, "I'm gonna kill this highbinder. When I do, if this gun-happy weak-brain shoots me, you put a slug into his guts."

"No," Butram said and walked to his horse and mounted, keeping his hands away from his guns.

Staring at Vent, who was watching the big rancher narrowly in an attempt to read his next move, Taper said, "You live a little longer, gunfighter . . . just a little longer." Then he turned to Caudell and, nodding his head at Vent as he slipped the Greener back in its scabbard, said, "Tie his hands," and mounted and rode out.

Stepping into the saddle, Vent patiently waited while Caudell tied his wrists behind his back. Catching the man's eye, he said simply, "Thanks, that ain't my favorite way of dying."

"You're welcome. I hope hanging is," Caudell said flatly and led his horse onto the wagon road.

Chapter IX

A summer rain had just swept through Dry Springs, leaving the dust dampened and the wooden sidewalks glistening, as the sun, once more king of the desert, blasted them to dryness with 110 degree heat. Out in the wash country south of town, water roared down narrow desert channels to spread in a wet sheet over the low spots, then quickly vanished as the sand drank it away.

Taper and his men rounded into the head of the street. The rancher had deliberately placed himself out in front with Vent's horse trailing behind him and Vent's bridle reins looped over his saddle horn.

Harp Sinclair moved onto the sidewalk in front of his place and leaned against a roof support, a broom straw stuck in the corner of his mouth. He watched the cavalcade come down the street and his face showed nothing.

The door of the Jinglebob Cafe swung open, and Carl Shipley came out carrying a pan of dirty dishwater, which he hurled into the street. Starting to turn back, he stopped when Sinclair called his name and nodded toward the livery stable. Turning then, Shipley saw Taper and the trussed-up Vent.

"Look at his face," Sinclair called.

Shipley stared at each man in turn and called back, "He didn't come easy."

The one-legged livery stable operator came to the door of his barn, stared at the passing riders, then turned his head and called to someone in the barn and was immediately joined by the blacksmith. The Wells Fargo stationmaster came out of his office and, leaning against the front of the building, had his look, shook his head, and went back inside.

The telegrapher, on his way to the Jinglebob Cafe for his breakfast, stopped short as he rounded into the main street from the railroad depot and then turned and retraced his steps.

As Taper reached the Red Horse Saloon, he rounded on Sinclair and said loudly, "This here's the pistol fighter who murdered my son. Here's the feller all you boys thought was so tough. Well, he ain't tough now and he's gonna be buzzard bait at sunup tomorrow 'cause that's when I'm gonna stretch his neck. Any you folks here in town wanta come watch the show, they'll be refreshments afterward, and the drinks will be on the D-Ring-T."

Turning his head, Vent looked at Caudell and said mildly, "Reckon this here windbag's gonna talk me to death."

Caudell looked away. Butram grinned openly, as did Shorty Hodge and Tuck Willoby. Taper, seeing this, jerked his horse around and, without another word, led his men toward the ranch.

As the big rancher rode past the last adobe on the street and lifted his horse to a hard trot south of Dry Springs, Harp Sinclair crossed the street and entered the Jinglebob, where he found his swamper, Shoe Slocum, sitting at the counter eating a stack of hotcakes drenched in syrup, and Shipley behind it drinking coffee and staring at the ragged Slocum in disgust.

Sinclair walked over to Slocum and, reaching down, grabbed him by the shirt front and dragged him off the stool and out to the front door. Hurling the swamper into the dirt, Sinclair drew his Colt and leveled it at the frightened man's head and snarled, "You got one way to stay alive, you slimy snake. You git . . . Just git. Outta town and don't stop. You've sold out the last man you're ever gonna sell out in this town . . ."

As the swamper rose shakily and started away, he said over his shoulder, "I'm gonna tell Mr. Taper you met that Leatherhand last night, and he'll come in here and kill you and burn this town to the ground."

Shaking his head, Shipley went back inside holstering his gun as he left the street, and looking at Sinclair, said, "I would dearly love to figure out where things like that come from."

"Hell, Carl, they just kinda fester under a cow pie until the sun hits 'em, then they pop out full-growed and start right out doing mischief," Sinclair said.

Down street Shoe Slocum was just entering the livery stable. As he stepped into the semidark interior, he called the blacksmith's name. When he got no answer, he climbed a ladder to the loft and began piling his meager belongings into an old coat, mumbling all the while to himself.

"Hello, little man," Sharp said as he stepped from behind a pile of hay.

Slocum jumped, then, seeing who his visitor was, he turned back and, ignoring him, went on packing. As he fastened the bundle together by simply tying the sleeves, Sharp suddenly sprang, whipped a long arm around the man's neck and, with a savage wrench, broke it. Then Sharp dragged his limp victim to the opening of the loft and hurled him into the street, where he landed with a dust-stirring thump.

As people ran toward the dead man, Sharp quietly clambered down the ladder and slipped out the rear. Walking along an alley until he was behind the Red Horse, Sharp cut around the building, and while half the town was occupied in standing around Slocum's body, he quickly entered the cafe.

"What's going on out there?" Sinclair, who was peering through the front window, asked.

Sharp went behind the counter and poured a cup of coffee and said mildly, "Seems that swamper feller took a header out the loft door down at the livery. Snapped the poor feller's neck like a dry stick."

Spencer, who had come in from the back of the cafe, stopped and stared at Sharp, as did the others, then shook his head and observed, "Just shows you a man can't be too careful where he steps."

"Serves him right," Sinclair said. "After Vent left last night I saw him walking south down the alley. Must have been hidden around somewhere and slipped over to the Red Horse. Tipped off Taper."

"That's the way I figured it," Sharp said. "It was him that sent Taper out to May's the first time too."

Spencer looked at the gambler for a moment, wondering how he had discovered that, then went back to eating a bowl of stew.

"So they figure on hanging Vent at dawn, do they?" Sharp mused. "Well, I reckon we'll just have to introduce a joker in that deck."

Spencer rose and, carrying his bowl and spoon, walked to the window and peered out. The townspeople were just in the process of lifting the limp body of the swamper onto a wooden door. As they raised the body, the head flopped loosely on its scrawny neck. Spencer turned away and sat down.

While the mortician, who doubled as the town's dentist, was busy laying Slocum's sorry remains out in a cheap wooden box, Taper led his men up over a low rise five miles from his ranch and raised his hand. The riders pulled in behind him, bunching up briefly, then spread out and watched a lone horseman coming toward them from the west.

When he hit the road, he turned left and came on, riding up to within thirty feet of Taper, and called, "You Grey Taper?"

"I am," Taper said, narrowly watching the man, who looked vaguely familiar.

"Name's Concho," the rider said. "Worked for Hazen Branda. He's dead. Killed by the Doolin bitch right in his own saloon. Boots Thomas, sided by that gambler, Owney Sharp, and your old foreman, Cam Spencer, shot the hell outta the Devil's Rondeevoo, killed the apron and two of Branda's boys. Thomas shut the place down, locked her tight."

"What happened to Hanks?" Taper asked.

"Apaches got him out near Two Guns," the man said. "Awful thing. They cut him up something fearsome. Left him hanging for the buzzards. Damn animals . . ."

Suddenly Butram spun his horse and rode back a little way and then stopped and called, "Rider from town, Mr. Taper."

Vent, watching Concho, noticed he favored his shoulder and recalled him as the man hit by the ricochet at the waterhole.

Taper rode back to join Butram, leading Vent's horse behind him.

"It's the livery man, old Pegleg," Butram said and watched as the one-legged man, his wooden member thrust out over the stirrup, came up on them at an awkward gallop, slopping from side to side in the old McClellan saddle he rode.

He drew rein in front of Taper and, looking at Vent for a moment, jerked his head back when the rancher snapped, "Well, Pegleg, you didn't come all the way out here just to look at this damn peckerwood. What the hell you want?"

The livery-stable owner looked at the ground then up at Taper and said, "Somebody broke Slocum's neck. Heaved him outta the loft . . ."

Staring at him, Taper said disgustedly, "You mean to say you rode all the way out here just to tell me some damn swamper got his neck busted. Man, you've been out in the sun too long."

"That ain't all," Pegleg said sullenly. "I figure it was Owney Sharp who killed him; Spencer's hanging around town too."

"The hell," Taper growled. "Don't mean nothing. Henry Brown's looking for those two. Seems he's got a warrant out of Kansas for them. He'll either take them back in handcuffs or dead."

"It ain't gonna go that way," the livery man said. "Stage driver told me yesterday he saw Brown way the-hell and gone over toward the New Mexico border . . . on my horse."

"Damn! Another lily-livered coward, and he stole my money," Taper snarled.

Vent grinned. "He stopped to tell me so long," he said, watching the wave of red sweep over the rancher's features as he whipped around and stared at his prisoner.

"That's a damn lie," he said.

"Nope. He asked me if I was planning to take a hand. I told him if he went after Owney or Cam, I'd kill him. He believed me. Said if I saw you to thank you for the money."

"Why that . . ." Taper swore then clamped his jaws shut. Whirling his horse, he jerked Vent after him, almost unseating him, and rode to the front of his men. Without looking back, he headed for the ranch at a fast trot.

When they quartered into the yard, Vent had his look, noting the tents around the perimeter and the blackened adobe walls of the ranch house thrusting up from the barren sod. The barn looked like some Civil War painting in which invading troops had put all to the torch and rode away. Then his eyes fell on the ancient oak standing alone in the center of the yard, its upper branches burned. Thrusting out from one side was a huge limb, and measuring it with his eye, Vent figured it was in just the right spot to use as a gallows.

Taper, watching him, said, "Take a good look at her, gunfighter. Tomorrow you'll be hanging from that big limb."

Looking at the rancher, Vent, his eyes cold and expressionless, said quietly, "It ain't tomorrow yet."

Laughing deep in his throat, Taper called Butram over and ordered him to tie Vent's feet and put a two-man guard on him.

Throwing a leg over the saddle swell, Vent dropped to the ground and followed Butram across the fire-blistered yard to where a corral post was still standing. He sat down with his back to it, looked up at the foreman, and asked, "Reckon this'll suit the big hee-haw?"

"You know, Torrey, you may just succeed in pushing him too far if you keep up that kinda stuff," Butram said.

"Not as long as he has this obsession about hanging me to that there oak," Vent said and looked at the ugly old tree.

Butram, having tied a rope around Vent's waist,

looped it around the post several times before tying it off. Sluicing an arm across his sweaty forehead, he looked at the oak and observed, "Anybody else would have cut that thing down years ago."

Half an hour later Caudell came by and checked Vent's ropes, then called over two riders and told them, "Watch this feller. Don't talk to him. Just watch him."

After he went away, one of the men, a lanky, cadaverous individual with an underslung jaw and a fist-flattened nose, squatted in the shade of a nearby tent and began whittling on a piece of wood. A Texan, he bragged he was the only man found not guilty in hanging judge Roy Bean's court at Pecos, Texas. His name was Sylvester, but he had long ago shortened it to Syl.

The second man was as broad as he was tall. Vent looked him over and wondered where Taper had dug him up from. The man stood six feet four, weighed 230 pounds, and when he shoved his battered hat back from his forehead, Vent could see he wore his hair cut almost to the skin. His face was wide and sharp as a broadaxe, and on one cheek there was a scar that could have been made by that selfsame broadaxe. His name was Elmo Grubbs, and he was the kind of man who, if angry, would run right down the twin bores of a shotgun, and to hell with the consequences.

Looking at them, Vent thought, With this pair, if I can't figure a way out of this by morning, I oughta hang. But each time he cast about for a way out, he drew a blank. The plan had to be simple because his guards were simpleminded. They wouldn't pick up on something the least bit subtle. Tired of racking his brain, Vent finally leaned back against the post and, tilting his head on his chest, dozed off. When he awoke an hour later, the sun was drilling down from directly above at better than 100 degrees. He was covered with sweat and felt just a little dizzy.

He must have dozed off again, because he didn't hear Caudell approach until he called the guards over and ordered them to rig a shelter over Vent's makeshift prison. Once a shelter half was in place and some of the power of the sun deflected, he felt better, but he had developed a raging thirst. When he asked for a drink, the Texan came over and held a canteen for him while he drank. The man did not speak, and when Vent had his fill, he capped the canteen and strolled back and flopped down in his original position. Just like a dog, Vent thought.

By the time the sun began its long slide down the other side of the world toward darkness, Vent's arms were numb. They had left his wrists tied. The rope Butram had lashed him to the post with was not tied to his arms. Thinking about that, he began carefully moving his arms around, but was forced to stop when a change in position brought a rush of blood to them and drove shooting darts of pain along his forearms. Once the pain subsided, he was back at it again, discovering he could move his arms a good five inches within the confines of the rope binding him to the post, but he couldn't shake the wrist lashings.

As the sun made its final plunge, Caudell came over carrying a plate and, handing it to Grubbs, said gruffly, "Feed the man," and went away.

Grubbs came over and spooned beans and bacon into Vent's mouth, then held a biscuit while he ate that. He was allowed to top it off with a cup of coffee and another drink of water; then the huge puncher, having accomplished all this without speaking one word, took the eating utensils away and returned again to squat in the yard and draw lines in the dust with a stick.

The big man amazed Vent. All day long he had squatted in the sun and, hat shading his eyes, drawn lines in the dust. Not once did he seek shade, as his partner had. Damn brain's probably boiled, Vent thought.

As Vent dozed under the makeshift tent, Taper came over, kicked his boot, and, smiling meanly, said, "Just had a nice steak dinner, topped off with a burgundy wine. Damn good too. Sorry about the miserable last meal, but what the hell, I ate for you." He threw back his head and roared with laughter.

"That's all right," Vent drawled. "My appetite just kinda went south right after I saw you out at May's old cabin. By the way, what did you do to her?"

"Told her to leave the country," Taper said. Then, face darkening, he observed, "If I had known what I know now, I'd've hanged her on that limb right alongside you. The two of you could go waltzing through hell together."

"When I get there, I'll tell Branda and Hanks you'll be along shortly, unless you beat me there," Vent said solemnly, looking off toward the east as if he could read it in the darkening sky.

"Now, what the hell you mean by that?" Taper asked, looking around uneasily.

Still scared of me, Vent thought, then looking directly at him, said, "You better start wearing armor, 'cause you're gonna be the target of a rifle fulla slugs from the time my horse walks out from under me to the day they pound dirt in your face."

"Hell, you think I'm worried about them friends of yours? It'll be the other way around. As soon as you stop kicking, we'll go look them up and weight them down with enough lead to start a lead mine."

"I don't think so, Mr. Taper. Them boys is pretty smart, and, Cam Spencer, he knows you like he knows his Colt. You never saw the day you could get up early enough in the morning to outfox that sly dog."

"I made him foreman because he knew cattle, but he proved he had no bottom for the long haul, so I fired him," Taper said.

"He left you because you murdered your friend, the marshal, and he couldn't gut a man who'd do that. They was no firing, Mr. Taper. He just rode out on you."

"Be that as it may, he'll be dead damn quick after you get yours," Taper retorted. As he turned and walked away, he called over his shoulder, "Ever see a man hanged, Mr. Leatherhand? He just sorta gags and jerks his knees way up in his chest and pulls his arms around trying to get loose. Face turns purple and the blood vessels start busting. When he kicks off, he craps his pants and pees all over himself. Ugly sight," and the rancher's laugh echoed back from the semidarkness as he moved in among the tents.

"Mean bastard," said Caudell, who had come up quietly.

"Not mean, Mr. Caudell. Crazy as a Piaute squaw on loco weed."

"Probably," Caudell agreed and, rolling a cigarette, stuck it in Vent's mouth and fired it up. As the sharp bite of the smoke struck his lungs, Vent realized how much he wanted to live. He didn't know how he was going to do it, but tomorrow he swore he would not hang from that damn oak tree.

"How come you stick to a man like Taper?" Vent asked curiously.

Caudell thought about it for a while then, removing Vent's cigarette, said musingly, "Feller gets his feet on the skids and just sorta keeps scrambling as he slides in deeper until finally he's there for fair unless something happens to let him get off."

Understanding Caudell perfectly, Vent said, "Man winds up behind a fast gun the same way."

"They say you could beat Hickok?"

"They say, but I don't know. I do know I've never had a man even come close to beating me," Vent said, and it was almost as if he were talking to himself.

Looking off toward where the oak tree stood stark against a moonswept desert, Caudell observed dryly, "That ain't no way for a man like you to go out," and rose and walked away.

Watching him fade into the darkness, Vent wondered if maybe the man might decide to take a hand at the last minute, then remembered Butram. If Caudell tried to interfere, Butram would kill him, Vent knew, and he would still hang. To hell with it, he thought, and went to sleep.

When he again awoke, it was just the beginning of a false morning when the first faint light of day comes and goes, plunging the world into a deep blackness that holds until the sun starts its upward swing. Then the voice spoke.

"I'm going to untie your hands, but I'll leave the rope around you," Sharp said, and Vent felt a great rush of relief as he looked over his shoulder at the dark shape kneeling behind him. Sharp, talking in a whisper, went on. "Me and Spencer are just beyond the camp loaded for bear. Harp and Carl taken a stand over behind the barn in a little ravine. They got rifles and they can sweep the whole damn yard . . . How many men's Taper got?"

"I count nine," Vent said, "Watch Butram. He's good and he's fast. Caudell is probably the most dangerous, but he ain't got no stomach for this. He could go any direction."

"Just so," Sharp whispered, then added, "I can give you a gun. How do you want to work this?"

Thinking it over, Vent whispered, "Taper will insist on putting the noose over my head, so he'll lead me to the oak. On the way I'll shuck outta these ropes and lift his gun. From then on the waltz begins."

"Sounds good, but you better drop off that horse fast, because that yard's gonna belong to no man in a damned big hurry when this starts."

Then the ropes were loose and Sharp had faded away behind him. Vent waited.

The camp began to stir as the sun lifted up over the edge of the horizon. Vent watched Taper come from the tent and then saw he was carrying a rope with a hangnoose tied in it.

Ordering his horse saddled, Taper walked to the oak and stood looking up at the branch. When he turned toward Vent, he had a wide smile on his face.

Butram led the horse up, and Taper mounted it and rode beneath the limb and tied the hang rope securely to the limb. Grasping it with both hands, he slid from his horse, hung for a moment, then dropped to the ground, leaving the rope swinging gently in the breeze, its noose gaping wide for Vent's neck.

Pointing to the Missourian, Taper said harshly, "Get him unroped and on a horse. Leave his hands tied." He remounted as his men came from the tents and stood staring at the dangling rope.

Vent placed Caudell standing just to the left of the burned-out shell of the adobe ranch house. Butram was moving out into the yard as Vent's two guards lifted him aboard the buckskin and stepped away.

"Nice knowing you," Grubbs said, and when Vent looked down at him sharply, there was no malice on his face. He had meant it.

Taper came over and picked up the buckskin's reins and began cakewalking his horse toward the oak tree.

"The last ride, gunfighter," he said, but there was no sarcasm in the statement. It was as if even this man who walked on the border of madness felt a certain mystery in what was about to transpire here.

The buckskin was moving chin-even with Taper's horse's flank when Vent gigged him lightly with his right-hand spur and moved him up beside the big rancher. In that split second he shook free of the ropes, jerked Taper's gun from its holster, and, whipping it up and around the rancher's head and shoulders, brought it to bear on Butram, who was even then dropping into a crouch and drawing his gun. Vent's first bullet shattered the man's gun arm. Butram executed the border shift, passing the weapon from his shattered right to his left just as Vent shot him through the chest, killing him instantly.

As Butram dropped, Vent whirled to place Taper and saw his horse running full tilt toward the oak tree. Dropping off the right side of the buckskin, Vent hit the ground in a crouch just as Sinclair and Shipley swept the yard with a savage burst of rifle fire and Sharp and Spencer cut down on the men near the tents from behind the wall of the blasted adobe.

Caudell, caught between two fires, dove behind the well house and emptied his guns in a vicious roll of thunder that was so fast it pushed one shot on top of another until they sounded as one continuous report.

Driven to ground, Sharp and Spencer held their fire until Caudell burned his last cap, then opened up on the well house, blasting away splinters of wood that whistled and sang all over the yard.

"Ah God, I'm hit," one of the riders shouted and ran

several steps into the yard and collapsed, his hand clasped to a spreading stain on his stomach.

Vent caught the skinny Texan in his sights as the man ran for cover in the barn ruins, and blew him off his feet. Whipped sideways by the impact of the heavy .45 slug, the man went into the air and smashed down in the dust on his back and lay still. Swinging the Colt, Vent aligned the sights on Grubbs, who was standing in the middle of the yard with his gun still in its holster, hesitated, then moved on in search of another target. When he glanced back Grubbs was still standing there.

"Grubbs, get the hell outta the yard!" Vent yelled and only then did the big man break and run. Vent watched as he dropped his head between his shoulders and raced wildly toward the desert. He was almost clear of the yard when Sharp suddenly stepped out in front of him and raised his gun.

Seeing the blank look on the big man's face, Sharp hesitated, then turned and dropped back into cover. Well, I'll be damned, Vent thought, he's slipping. Then Caudell was shouting for the D-Ring-T men to hold their fire.

When the echoes of the last shot faded across the desert, Caudell called out, "No need for any more of this. Look at the oak."

All eyes turned toward the hanging tree. Dangling from the noose Taper had prepared so lovingly for Vent was the rancher himself. Vent rose and walked over, and, gun hanging loosely in his hand, stared up at the big man and wondered.

Caudell had come up behind Vent, as had Sharp and Spencer, and now he said quietly, "Without a boss, they's no pay. Me, I don't fight for nothing."

Shorty Hodge walked up on his bowed legs, took a stance under the tree, cocked his head to one side, and observed, "He sure looks peaceful hangin' there, don't he?"

"What ya reckon happened?" one of Taper's men asked. He was nursing a smashed left arm.

"Looks to me like his horse run him in under the tree and he just got his head caught in the noose," Caudell guessed.

"Well, I'll be damned," Sinclair said. He and Shipley had come up and were standing behind the Taper riders staring at the grisly fruit dangling from the oak limb.

"What'd the feller say? Poetic justice . . ." Sharp mused.

Turning away, the men tramped off to doctor their injuries as Caudell and Vent went to the well. As Vent stared at the riddled well house, Caudell pulled up a bucket full of water and drank directly from the pail. Handing it to Vent he said, "Reckon it feels kinda good to be able to swallow this morning."

"How the hell did you stay alive behind that well house?" Vent asked.

"I'm from Missouri. You oughta know we folks from old Misery got luck. We may not have money, we usually ain't too smart, and we damn sure make more than our share of mistakes, but we do got luck."

"Riders coming," one of Taper's men called.

All eyes turned to the Dry Springs road as a cavalry patrol came smartly over the rise led by a tall, gaunt officer on a white horse. As they came on at a hard trot, the officer called out sharply, "Look smart there. Sergeant, keep them straightened up."

Vent walked out into the middle of the yard buckling on his .44, resurrected from Taper's tent. The Appaloosa, saddled and ready, had been brought from town by Harp Sinclair, and now he stood tied to the fence post that had served as Vent's prison during the night.

The officer led his troop into the edge of the yard, held up his hand, and called sharply, "Troop, halt!"

Sitting his horse ramrod straight, he looked at the swinging body of Grey Taper hanging from the oak and then down at Vent and said, "Well, Mr. Torrey, it seems we meet again."

"Major Bedlam, sir, it's good to see you," Vent replied.

The officer smiled and, touching his shoulder boards, said, "It's colonel now, Mr. Torrey."

"Congratulations, sir. Couldn't have happened to a more deserving officer."

Sharp came up then, and Vent turned and, nodding at the colonel, said, "This here's Major . . . Colonel Royce C. Bedlam, Seventh Cavalry. We met out in Kansas and the colonel was exceedingly kind to me and my family. Colonel, meet Owney Sharp."

Saluting the gambler, Bedlam said, "Pleased, suh," and turning his head, shouted, "Sergeant, front and center."

A heavyset trooper wearing chevrons on his sleeve came forward and, wheeling his horse in front of the colonel, saluted sharply and said, "Sir?"

"Get crowbars. Go to work on those walls," the colonel ordered as Vent watched, puzzled.

The sergeant tolled off four men, who immediately dismounted and pulled large crowbars from a pack horse. They went to the adobe and began prying blocks loose around the fireplace. While they worked, the colonel ordered his men to be at ease and, dismounting, walked over to the slowly twisting body. He gazed up into Taper's congested face and asked, "You hang him?"

"No sir. It was an accident," Vent answered, and he told the colonel the basics of what had been happening in the Verde Valley.

"So he sought to hang you and died on his own rope,"

Bedlam mused. "Well, that's not surprising. Captain Grey Taper was born to end like this. If you hadn't done the job, the army would have. You saved the taxpayers some money."

A shout from the adobe interrupted them, and turning, the colonel walked briskly to the wall, looked over it, and said, "Open it, Sergeant."

Vent came up as the sergeant heaved a heavy strong-box over the wall. It landed in the dust of the yard with a thump, and one of the troopers immediately jammed his crowbar under the lid. Snapping the lock, he flipped it back. There were gasps from the Taper riders as they stared at the gleaming box full of gold coins. Stepping back, the colonel said, "You men are looking at part of a payroll robbery perpetrated by the late Captain Taper. He and two sergeants, Hanks and Branda, hit a pay wagon on its way to Fort San Antonio. They got away clean."

"Well, I'll be damned," Caudell said, staring at the gold.

"And so will I," Shorty Hodge echoed.

"A damn holdup artist," one of the Taper riders marveled.

"And in the army too," another said.

Bedlam turned smartly then and said, "Sergeant, load this on a pack animal and let's move it out."

Mounting his horse, he rode back and looked down at Vent and said, "Everywhere I go, I hear the name Leatherhand. The last time I saw you that right hand couldn't hold a gun, let alone fire it. Now you're rated with some pretty fast people. Someday we'll meet again and you'll tell me how it all happened."

"It'll be my pleasure," Vent promised and watched as the colonel ordered his men into formation and moved out smartly on the Dry Springs road.

Turning to Caudell, Vent asked, "Any plans, Mr. Caudell?"

"Another ranch, another boss," Caudell said.

"Pick the next outfit carefully," Vent counseled. "You're too good a man for this kind of thing." Then he looked up and asked curiously, "Would you have let Taper hang me?"

Caudell turned and walked off, then stopped and looked back and said, "Hell no," and went to his horse and rode out.

Epilogue

In the next two weeks, Colonel Royce C. Bedlam led his troop across the Verde Valley and made two stops, each time riding away with a strongbox full of gold coins. When the colonel's mission was completed, he rode from the Verde Valley and did not look back.

Lud McKiver did not propose to Amelia Jorstad, but a little thing like that couldn't stop a woman who had bested the Apache Kid. She proposed to him. The wedding was one of the biggest in the Verde Valley, and the rimrock echoed the lively fiddle music for two days as the celebrants danced away the hours and toasted the bride and groom with stocks of liquor provided by Marshal Boots Thomas, liquor he said he had confiscated from a saloon he had shut down.

No one came to claim the D-Ring-T, and eventually it disappeared from the brand books, but the old oak tree stood in the yard overlooking the crumbling adobe walls of one man's dreams for fifty years before a summer storm sent a lightning bolt to splinter it to its very roots.

Said Harp Sinclair's son, who had inherited the Red Dog Saloon from his father, "Probably old Grey Taper come back to take final revenge on that old oak tree on account of it hanging him."

Cam Spencer became Dry Springs's new marshal, and one day as he and Sharp sat on the front porch of his office, chairs tilted against the jailhouse wall, the man called Leatherhand rode down the street and stopped and had his look.

"Better drift along, gunfighter," the marshal said. "We don't need your kind in Dry Springs."

The gambler, his clothes showing no dust even though the wind was kicking up dust devils in the street, cocked his hat over his eyes and said solemnly, "Best be careful, marshal. There sits the hombre that hung Grey Taper."

"So I heard," the marshal said. "Wonder where he's headed." Then Spencer looked up and asked, "Where you headed, Mr. Leatherhand?"

Vent Torrey grinned. "Across the mountain to see where the sun goes," he said and clucked up the big Appaloosa.

"Just so," the marshal said.

"Keep a tight cinch and a fistful of aces," the gambler counseled.

The man called Leatherhand did not answer, merely lifted his leather-bound hand and waved.